THE MODERN LIBRARY TORCHBEARERS

THE GOODNESS
OF ST. ROCQUE

THE GOODNESS OF ST. ROCQUE

AND OTHER STORIES

ALICE DUNBAR-NELSON

Introduction by Danielle Evans

THE MODERN LIBRARY

NEW YORK

2022 Modern Library Trade Paperback Edition
Introduction copyright © 2022 by Danielle Evans

Published in the United States by The Modern Library, an imprint of Random House, a division of Penguin Random House LLC, New York.

The Modern Library and the Torchbearer colophon are registered trademarks of Penguin Random House LLC.

Some of the stories in this work were originally published in *Violets and Other Tales* by Alice Dunbar-Nelson.

ISBN 978-0-593-24407-4
Ebook ISBN 978-0-593-24408-1

Printed in the United States of America on acid-free paper

modernlibrary.com
randomhousebooks.com

1st Printing

To
My best Comrade
My Husband

CONTENTS

SELECTED STORIES FROM
VIOLETS AND OTHER TALES

INTRODUCTION
DANIELLE EVANS

_____

Some twenty years after the publication of her short-story collection _The Goodness of St. Rocque and Other Stories_, Alice Dunbar-Nelson began to keep a regular diary. She opened with "Had I enough sense to keep a diary all these years I have been traveling around...well, there would be less confusion in my mind about lots of things. Now I begin this day to keep the record that should have been kept long since." In rereading these stories, I've been thinking about that Alice Dunbar-Nelson: the woman who fretted over her legacy, nursed private griefs and disappointments, wrestled in her personal life with the tension between respectable restraint and raucous joy and honesty. In the title story, Dunbar-Nelson writes, "For your creole girls are proud and would die rather than let the world see their sorrows," and one does get the sense that this is a pride Dunbar-Nelson knew intimately. That tension between the desire to be seen, sorrows and all, and the terror of achieving that kind of honest visibility is at the center of so much of her writing, and her anxieties about its reception.

Dunbar-Nelson kept that diary, part deliberate record, part private chronicle of her inner life, for at least a decade. It displays much of what her more public writing does about her singular voice—a wry sense of humor, a talent for capturing in vivid language the way the natural world can mirror or illuminate human feeling, a complex sense of what motivates people, an eye for hypocrisy, frustration with being at the mercy of people who don't know what they're doing and with having to adhere to expectations of decorum or respectability or feminine charm in her responses. It also documents the things that didn't explicitly make it into her published work, including her insecurities, romantic affairs with men and women outside of her marriages, and a litany of grievances, ranging from structural to petty.

Despite Dunbar-Nelson's efforts at documentation, the historical record hasn't always quite known what to do with her. A prolific writer who published her first book at nineteen, Dunbar-Nelson was a poet, fiction writer, essayist, and newspaper columnist; a writer whose career spanned the post-Reconstruction era and the Harlem Renaissance; a writer whose impressive work as an artist and activist never quite lived up to her own standards for herself and never let her escape her worry that her legacy wouldn't be enough; a serious and self-driven artist whose body of work is still sometimes discussed primarily in relation to her first husband, Paul Laurence Dunbar, though it was, in part, her writing that drew them together in the first place. In "Recovering Alice Dunbar-Nelson for the Twenty-First Century: An Introduction," Katharine Adams, Sandra Zagarell, and Caroline Gebhard write of Dunbar-Nelson, "Her marriage to Paul Laurence Dunbar was, for years, the only thing making her visible and the primary thing obscuring her from view."

In both its content and its existence as public document, Dunbar-Nelson's diary (edited by Akasha Gloria Hull and published by Norton in 1984) reflects some of the ambiguities of her life and career. It is one of only a few early private records we have of the inner life of a Black woman writer in the United States; part of the reason we have it is that scholars valued the insight Dunbar-Nelson's papers might provide about her first husband. In a culture that likes to reduce Black writers to digestible trivia facts and women and queer writers to their personal associations, a queer Black woman writer whose work doesn't lend itself to a summarizing sentence poses a challenge when considered on her own terms.

Though it means her other works are comparatively underread, it feels fitting to me that Dunbar-Nelson's best-known book is a story collection. Good story collections by their nature resist reductive readings; the short story is a comfortable home for a writer evading being boxed in or pinned down. A collection may be tied to a region, or circle a thematic question, but it's hard to reduce a collection to a thesis, to say a single meaningful thing that is true of every one of a writer's stories when a collection so often sits contrasting or even contradictory voices beside one another. In a landscape often committed to reading the work of marginalized writers as pure autobiography or polemic, the story collection often forces a critical conversation that takes marginalized writers' craft seriously, that must reckon with ambiguity and contradiction. On their own, some of Dunbar-Nelson's stories do feel unambiguous, framed to lead the reader to a neat moral lesson or philosophical conclusion, but setting these stories next to the rest of her work makes them interestingly messier.

Dunbar-Nelson is a beautiful observer of the world; despite her lament that she began recording things too late for her personal purposes, this collection does its own kind of record keeping. New Orleans is its principal recurring character; Dunbar-Nelson portrays a vibrant multiethnic city, full of neighborhoods where characters from different backgrounds might cross paths, as well as insular neighborhoods where the rest of the city might as well be a world away. In the present moment, it is of course obvious the ways in which New Orleans is vulnerable to drastic change, the way plans to correct or improve it lay bare its structural inequities; here, just before the turn of the twentieth century, Dunbar-Nelson recognizes that the communities she's writing about are frequently at the mercy of "the ruthless vandalism of the improving idea." Dunbar-Nelson is interested in equal parts in landscape and character, though the landscape often takes on the mood of the story. The lush reeds surrounding a pair of young lovers are in fact "False reeds! They tell themselves of their happiness to be, and it all ends in dry stalks and drizzling skies." The trees of New Orleans are forthright and urgent about their business, for "down here the trees do not swell and bud slowly and tease you for weeks with promises of greenness."

People are often part of the landscape, too, and one of the fascinating things about this book is how often Dunbar-Nelson is interested not just in telling the reader what happened, but telling the reader how it will be talked or gossiped about after the fact. The delicious ambiguity of the ending of "The Goodness of St. Rocque" rests on Dunbar-Nelson having an impeccable sense of when to intervene with omniscience and when to sit multiple versions of a story next to one another, choosing polyphony over resolution.

In this way, throughout the collection, Dunbar-Nelson is able to center individual voices while reminding the reader that they are part of a larger network. Like the characters at the end of "Mr. Baptiste," Dunbar-Nelson zooms in on "the individual, the concrete bit of helpless humanity," but only after thoroughly situating each person in a context and community such that we understand the position from which her characters move through the world. Interestingly, for all of the specificity of her New Orleans, and all of the stories she tells that feel possible only in its particular cultural milieu, in "Mr. Baptiste," Dunbar-Nelson decides to emphasize New Orleans as a place where, for all of its ethnic diversity and international influence, the racial logic of the United States prevails, making it prone to the same violence as everywhere else. (There were a series of labor strikes in New Orleans in the 1890s, and Dunbar-Nelson chooses to frame her story not around the 1892 general strike, famous for resisting the racial division and racist violence common to labor organizing at the time and winning a muted but unlikely multiracial victory, but on events during a later period, characterized by the kind of racial separatism and tragedy her story depicts, even for a character who can initially move freely across the color line.)

Frequently, the most interesting ambiguities in these stories stem from the tension between propriety and restlessness. In the stories included here from Dunbar-Nelson's earlier collection, *Violets and Other Tales,* her moral claims are more direct, but even then they are tempered by longing. The bohemian neighborhood in "Anarchy Alley" is "a veritable nursery of riot and disorder" but the reader is warned off and invited in in equal parts. In "The Bee-Man," a man is given the chance to enter an enchanted world, with the condition that the first thing he finds himself attached to will reveal his true self and give him a chance to start over. Interestingly, immediately after presenting this premise, the story chooses to ignore it—the bee-man immediately becomes "violently attached to the handsome person and fine castle of the Lord of the Realm"—but this attachment is dispensed with in a sentence and doesn't seem to count as fulfilling the terms of the agreement. The story's tidy ending is complicated by that earlier brief aside, hovering there un-resolved, an escape hatch to the neat resolution that leaves the reader wondering who the man might have been if he'd been allowed to love what he actually loved.

In the stories from *The Goodness of St. Rocque*, the moral and philosophical questions are a bit more nuanced, though there is danger in both respectability and its abandonment. A young girl at Carnival is assigned a playful disguise that turns the story ominous; another young woman enters a convent in a hurry, then determines that she's made a mis-take; a poor creole woman sacrifices what little she has to buy back from a pawn shop the ring a once-wealthy lover gave her. Dunbar-Nelson's sense of fate is less didactic in these later stories, but she remains interested in the ques-tion of what it means that doing the right thing can't save you. Fate isn't always against her characters; in her fiction, the world is capable of enormous indifference and also of unexpected kindness and generosity. Lost things—loves, violins—occasionally return. If the city she depicts is some-times mercurial, the reader can live in it as her characters do, not sure what happens next or how things will turn out, looking ahead and seeing possibility everywhere. That sense of possibility is what makes me settle in with her work, read-ing with the breathless anticipation I get when lost in a good story. Dunbar-Nelson's view of the world here is, it seems to me, neither optimistic nor pessimistic, but in search of a kind of mercy, hopeful that her recording of these lives of both sorrow and grace might bring us closer to it.

Danielle Evans

September 2021

—

DANIELLE EVANS is the author of the story collections *The Office of Historical Corrections* and *Before You Suffocate Your Own Fool Self*. Her first collection won the PEN/Robert W. Bingham Prize, the Hurston/Wright Legacy Award for fiction, and the Paterson Prize for fiction; her second was a finalist for the Aspen Prize, the Story Prize, the Chautauqua Prize, and the Los Angeles Times Book Prize for fiction. She is the 2021 winner of the New Literary Project's Joyce Carol Oates Prize, a 2020 National Endowment for the Arts fellow, and a 2011 National Book Foundation 5 Under 35 honoree. Her stories have appeared in magazines and anthologies including *The Best American Short Stories* and *New Stories from the South*. She teaches in The Writing Seminars at Johns Hopkins University.

THE GOODNESS
OF ST. ROCQUE

THE GOODNESS OF ST. ROCQUE

Manuela was tall and slender and graceful, and once you knew her the lithe form could never be mistaken. She walked with the easy spring that comes from a perfectly arched foot. To-day she swept swiftly down Marais Street, casting a quick glance here and there from under her heavy veil as if she feared she was being followed. If you had peered under the veil, you would have seen that Manuela's dark eyes were swollen and discoloured about the lids, as though they had known a sleepless, tearful night.

There had been a picnic the day before, and as merry a crowd of giddy, chattering Creole girls and boys as ever you could see boarded the ramshackle dummy-train that puffed its way wheezily out wide Elysian Fields Street, around the lily-covered bayous, to Milneburg-on-the-Lake. Now, a picnic at Milneburg is a thing to be remembered for ever. One charters a rickety-looking, weather-beaten dancing-pavilion, built over the water, and after storing the children—for your true Creole never leaves the small folks at home—and the baskets and mothers downstairs, the young folks go up-stairs and dance to the tune of the best band you ever heard. For what can equal the music of a violin, a guitar, a cornet, and a bass viol to trip the quadrille to at a picnic?

Then one can fish in the lake and go bathing under the prim bath-houses, so severely separated sexually, and go rowing on the lake in a trim boat, followed by the shrill warnings of anxious mamans. And in the evening one comes home, hat crowned with cool gray Spanish moss, hands burdened with fantastic latanier baskets woven by the brown bayou boys, hand in hand with your dearest one, tired but happy.

At this particular picnic, however, there had been bitterness of spirit. Theophilé was Manuela's own especial property, and Theophilé had proven false. He had not danced a single waltz or quadrille with Manuela, but had deserted her for Claralie, blonde and petite. It was Claralie whom Theophilé had rowed out on the lake; it was Claralie whom Theophilé had gallantly led to dinner; it was Claralie's hat that he wreathed with Spanish moss, and Claralie whom he escorted home after the jolly singing ride in town on the little dummy-train.

Not that Manuela lacked partners or admirers. Dear no! she was too graceful and beautiful for that. There had been more than enough for her. But Manuela loved Theophilé, you see, and no one could take his place. Still, she had tossed her head and let her silvery laughter ring out in the dance, as though she were the happiest of mortals, and had tripped home with Henri, leaning on his arm, and looking up into his eyes as though she adored him.

This morning she showed the traces of a sleepless night and an aching heart as she walked down Marais Street. Across wide St. Rocque Avenue she hastened. "Two blocks to the river and one below—" she repeated to herself breathlessly. Then she stood on the corner gazing about her, until with a final summoning of a desperate courage she dived through a small wicket gate into a garden of weed-choked flowers.

There was a hoarse, rusty little bell on the gate that gave querulous tongue as she pushed it open. The house that sat back in the yard was little and old and weather-beaten. Its one-story frame had once been painted, but that was a memory remote and traditional. A straggling morning-glory strove to conceal its time-ravaged face. The little walk of broken bits of brick was reddened carefully, and the one little step was scrupulously yellow-washed, which denoted that the occupants were cleanly as well as religious.

Manuela's timid knock was answered by a harsh "Entrez."

It was a small sombre room within, with a bare yellow-washed floor and ragged curtains at the little window. In a corner was a diminutive altar draped with threadbare lace. The red glow of the taper lighted a cheap print of St. Joseph and a brazen crucifix. The human element in the room was furnished by a little, wizened yellow woman, who, black-robed, turbaned, and stern, sat before an uncertain table whereon were greasy cards.

Manuela paused, her eyes blinking at the semi-obscurity within. The Wizened One called in croaking tones:

"An' fo' w'y you come here? Assiez-là, ma'amzelle."

Timidly Manuela sat at the table facing the owner of the voice.

"I want," she began faintly; but the Mistress of the Cards understood: she had had much experience. The cards were shuffled in her long grimy talons and stacked before Manuela.

"Now you cut dem in t'ree part, so—un, deux, trois, bien! You mek' you' weesh wid all you' heart, bien! Yaas, I see, I see!"

Breathlessly did Manuela learn that her lover was true, but "dat light gal, yaas, she mek' nouvena in St. Rocque fo' hees love."

"I give you one lil' charm, yaas," said the Wizened One when the séance was over, and Manuela, all white and nervous, leaned back in the rickety chair. "I give you one lil' charm fo' to ween him back, yaas. You wear h'it 'roun' you' wais', an' he come back. Den you mek prayer at St. Rocque an' burn can'le. Den you come back an' tell me, yaas. Cinquante sous, ma'amzelle. Merci. Good luck go wid you."

Readjusting her veil, Manuela passed out the little wicket gate, treading on air. Again the sun shone, and the breath of the swamps came as healthful sea-breeze unto her nostrils. She fairly flew in the direction of St. Rocque.

There were quite a number of persons entering the white gates of the cemetery, for this was Friday, when all those who wish good luck pray to the saint, and wash their steps promptly at twelve o'clock with a wondrous mixture to guard the house. Manuela bought a candle from the keeper of the little lodge at the entrance, and pausing one instant by the great sun-dial to see if the heavens and the hour were propitious, glided into the tiny chapel, dim and stifling with heavy air from myriad wish-candles blazing on the wide table before the altar-rail. She said her prayer and lighting her candle placed it with the others.

Mon Dieu! how brightly the sun seemed to shine now, she thought, pausing at the door on her way out. Her small finger-tips, still bedewed with holy water, rested caressingly on a gamin's head. The ivy which enfolds the quaint chapel never seemed so green; the shrines which serve as the Way of the Cross never seemed so artistic; the baby graves, even, seemed cheerful.

Theophilé called Sunday. Manuela's heart leaped. He

had been spending his Sundays with Claralie. His stay was short and he was plainly bored. But Manuela knelt to thank the good St. Rocque that night, and fondled the charm about her slim waist. There came a box of bonbons during the week, with a decorative card all roses and fringe, from Theophilé; but being a Creole, and therefore superstitiously careful, and having been reared by a wise and experienced maman to mistrust the gifts of a recreant lover, Manuela quietly thrust bonbons, box, and card into the kitchen fire, and the Friday following placed the second candle of her nouvena in St. Rocque.

Those of Manuela's friends who had watched with indignation Theophilé gallantly leading Claralie home from High Mass on Sundays, gasped with astonishment when the next Sunday, with his usual bow, the young man offered Manuela his arm as the worshippers filed out in step to the organ's march. Claralie tossed her head as she crossed herself with holy water, and the pink in her cheeks was brighter than usual.

Manuela smiled a bright good-morning when she met Claralie in St. Rocque the next Friday. The little blonde blushed furiously, and Manuela rushed post-haste to the Wizened One to confer upon this new issue.

"H'it ees good," said the dame, shaking her turbaned head. "She ees 'fraid, she will work, mais you' charm, h'it weel beat her."

And Manuela departed with radiant eyes.

Theophilé was not at Mass Sunday morning, and murderous glances flashed from Claralie to Manuela before the tinkling of the Host-Bell. Nor did Theophilé call at either house. Two hearts beat furiously at the sound of every passing footstep, and two minds wondered if the other were enjoying the beloved one's smiles. Two pair of eyes, however, blue and black, smiled on others, and their owners laughed and seemed none the less happy. For your Creole girls are proud, and would die rather than let the world see their sorrows.

Monday evening Theophilé, the missing, showed his rather sheepish countenance in Manuela's parlour, and explained that he, with some chosen spirits, had gone for a trip—"over the Lake."

"I did not ask you where you were yesterday," replied the girl, saucily.

Theophilé shrugged his shoulders and changed the conversation.

The next week there was a birthday fête in honour of Louise, Theophilé's young sister. Everyone was bidden, and no one thought of refusing, for Louise was young, and this would be her first party. So, though the night was hot, the dancing went on as merrily as light young feet could make it go. Claralie fluffed her dainty white skirts, and cast mischievous sparkles in the direction of Theophilé, who with the maman and Louise was bravely trying not to look self-conscious. Manuela, tall and calm and proud-looking, in a cool, pale yellow gown, was apparently enjoying herself without paying the slightest attention to her young host.

"Have I the pleasure of this dance?" he asked her finally, in a lull of the music.

She bowed assent, and as if moved by a common impulse they strolled out of the dancing-room into the cool, quaint garden, where jessamines gave out an overpowering perfume, and a caged mocking-bird complained melodiously to the full moon in the sky.

It must have been an engrossing tête-a-tête, for the call to supper had sounded twice before they heard and hurried into the house. The march had formed with Louise radiantly leading on the arm of papa. Claralie tripped by with Leon. Of course, nothing remained for Theophilé and Manuela to do but to bring up the rear, for which they received much good-natured chaffing.

But when the party reached the dining-room, Theophilé proudly led his partner to the head of the table, at the right hand of maman, and smiled benignly about at the delighted assemblage. Now you know, when a Creole young man places a girl at his mother's right hand at his own table, there is but one conclusion to be deduced therefrom.

If you had asked Manuela, after the wedding was over, how it happened, she would have said nothing, but looked wise.

If you had asked Claralie, she would have laughed and said she always preferred Leon.

If you had asked Theophilé, he would have wondered that you thought he had ever meant more than to tease Manuela.

If you had asked the Wizened One, she would have offered you a charm.

But St. Rocque knows, for he is a good saint, and if you believe in him and are true and good, and make your nouvenas with a clean heart, he will grant your wish.

TONY'S WIFE

"Gimme fi' cents worth o' candy, please." It was the little Jew girl who spoke, and Tony's wife roused herself from her knitting to rise and count out the multi-hued candy which should go in exchange for the dingy nickel grasped in warm, damp fingers. Three long sticks, carefully wrapped in crispest brown paper, and a half dozen or more of pink candy fish for lagniappe, and the little Jew girl sped away in blissful contentment. Tony's wife resumed her knitting with a stifled sigh until the next customer should come.

A low growl caused her to look up apprehensively. Tony himself stood beetle-browed and huge in the small doorway.

"Get up from there," he muttered, "and open two dozen oysters right away; the Eliots want 'em." His English was unaccented. It was long since he had seen Italy.

She moved meekly behind the counter, and began work on the thick shells. Tony stretched his long neck up the street.

"Mr. Tony, mama wants some charcoal." The very small voice at his feet must have pleased him, for his black brows relaxed into a smile, and he poked the little one's chin with a hard, dirty finger, as he emptied the ridiculously small bucket of charcoal into the child's bucket, and gave a banana for lagniappe.

The crackling of shells went on behind, and a stifled sob arose as a bit of sharp edge cut into the thin, worn fingers that clasped the knife.

"Hurry up there, will you?" growled the black brows; "the Eliots are sending for the oysters."

She deftly strained and counted them, and, after wiping her fingers, resumed her seat, and took up the endless crochet work, with her usual stifled sigh.

Tony and his wife had always been in this same little queer old shop on Prytania Street, at least to the memory of the oldest inhabitant in the neighbourhood. When or how they came, or how they stayed, no one knew; it was enough that they were there, like a sort of ancestral fixture to the street. The neighbourhood was fine enough to look down upon these two tumble-down shops at the corner, kept by Tony and Mrs. Murphy, the grocer. It was a semi-fashionable locality, far up-town, away from the old-time French quarter. It was the sort of neighbourhood where millionaires live before their fortunes are made and fashionable, high-priced private schools flourish, where the small cottages are occupied by aspiring school-teachers and choir-singers. Such was this locality, and you must admit that it was indeed a condescension to tolerate Tony and Mrs. Murphy.

He was a great, black-bearded, hoarse-voiced, six-foot specimen of Italian humanity, who looked in his little shop and on the prosaic pavement of Prytania Street somewhat as Hercules might seem in a modern drawing-room. You instinctively thought of wild mountain-passes, and the gleaming dirks of bandit contadini in looking at him. What his last name was, no one knew. Someone had maintained once that he had been christened Antonio Malatesta, but that was unauthentic, and as little to be believed as that other wild theory that her name was Mary.

She was meek, pale, little, ugly, and German. Altogether part of his arms and legs would have very decently made another larger than she. Her hair was pale and drawn in sleek, thin tightness away from a pinched, pitiful face, whose dull cold eyes hurt you, because you knew they were trying to mirror sorrow, and could not because of their expressionless quality. No matter what the weather or what her other toilet, she always wore a thin little shawl of dingy brick-dust hue about her shoulders. No matter what the occasion or what the day, she always carried her knitting with her, and seldom ceased the incessant twist, twist of the shining steel among the white cotton meshes. She might put down the needles and lace into the spool-box long enough to open oysters, or wrap up fruit and candy, or count out wood and coal into infinitesimal portions, or do her housework; but the knitting was snatched with avidity at the first spare moment, and the worn, white, blue-marked fingers, half enclosed in kid-glove stalls for protection, would writhe and twist in and out again. Little girls just learning to crochet borrowed their patterns from Tony's wife, and it was considered quite a mark of advancement to have her inspect a bit of lace done by eager, chubby fingers. The ladies in larger houses, whose husbands would be millionaires some day, bought her lace, and gave it to their servants for Christmas presents.

As for Tony, when she was slow in opening his oysters or in cooking his red beans and spaghetti, he roared at her, and prefixed picturesque adjectives to her lace, which made her hide it under her apron with a fearsome look in her dull eyes.

He hated her in a lusty, roaring fashion, as a healthy beefy boy hates a sick cat and torments it to madness. When she displeased him, he beat her, and knocked her frail form on the floor. The children could tell when this had happened. Her eyes would be red, and there would be blue marks on her face and neck. "Poor Mrs. Tony," they would say, and nestle close to her. Tony did not roar at her for petting them, perhaps, because they spent money on the multi-hued candy in glass jars on the shelves.

Her mother appeared upon the scene once, and stayed a short time; but Tony got drunk one day and beat her because she ate too much, and she disappeared soon after. Whence she came and where she departed, no one could tell, not even Mrs. Murphy, the Pauline Pry and Gazette of the block.

Tony had gout, and suffered for many days in roaring helplessness, the while his foot, bound and swathed in many folds of red flannel, lay on the chair before him. In proportion as his gout increased and he bawled from pure physical discomfort, she became light-hearted, and moved about the shop with real, brisk cheeriness. He could not hit her then without such pain that after one or two trials he gave up in disgust.

So the dull years had passed, and life had gone on pretty much the same for Tony and the German wife and the shop. The children came on Sunday evenings to buy the stick candy, and on week-days for coal and wood. The servants came to buy oysters for the larger houses, and to gossip over the counter about their employers. The little dry woman knitted, and the big man moved lazily in and out in his red flannel shirt, exchanged politics with the tailor next door through the window, or lounged into Mrs. Murphy's bar and drank fiercely. Some of the children grew up and moved away, and other little girls came to buy candy and eat pink lagniappe fishes, and the shop still thrived.

One day Tony was ill, more than the mummied foot of gout, or the wheeze of asthma; he must keep his bed and send for the doctor.

She clutched his arm when he came, and pulled him into the tiny room.

"Is it—is it anything much, doctor?" she gasped.

Æsculapius shook his head as wisely as the occasion would permit. She followed him out of the room into the shop.

"Do you—will he get well, doctor?"

Æsculapius buttoned up his frock coat, smoothed his shining hat, cleared his throat, then replied oracularly,

"Madam, he is completely burned out inside. Empty as a shell, madam, empty as a shell. He cannot live, for he has nothing to live on."

As the cobblestones rattled under the doctor's equipage rolling leisurely up Prytania Street, Tony's wife sat in her chair and laughed,—laughed with a hearty joyousness that lifted the film from the dull eyes and disclosed a sparkle beneath.

The drear days went by, and Tony lay like a veritable Samson shorn of his strength, for his voice was sunken to a hoarse, sibilant whisper, and his black eyes gazed fiercely from the shock of hair and beard about a white face. Life went on pretty much as before in the shop; the children paused to ask how Mr. Tony was, and even hushed the jingles on their bell hoops as they passed the door. Red-headed Jimmie, Mrs. Murphy's nephew, did the hard jobs, such as splitting wood and lifting coal from the bin; and in the intervals between tending the fallen giant and waiting on the customers, Tony's wife sat in her accustomed chair, knitting fiercely, with an inscrutable smile about her purple compressed mouth.

Then John came, introducing himself, serpent-wise, into the Eden of her bosom.

John was Tony's brother, huge and bluff too, but fair and blond, with the beauty of Northern Italy. With the same lack of race pride which Tony had displayed in selecting his German spouse, John had taken unto himself Betty, a daughter of Erin, aggressive, powerful, and cross-eyed. He turned up now, having heard of this illness, and assumed an air of remarkable authority at once.

A hunted look stole into the dull eyes, and after John had departed with blustering directions as to Tony's welfare, she crept to his bedside timidly.

"Tony," she said,—"Tony, you are very sick."

An inarticulate growl was the only response.

"Tony, you ought to see the priest; you mustn't go any longer without taking the sacrament."

The growl deepened into words.

"Don't want any priest; you 're always after some snivelling old woman's fuss. You and Mrs. Murphy go on with your church; it won't make *you* any better."

She shivered under this parting shot, and crept back into the shop. Still the priest came next day.

She followed him in to the bedside and knelt timidly.

"Tony," she whispered, "here's Father Leblanc."

Tony was too languid to curse out loud; he only expressed his hate in a toss of the black beard and shaggy mane.

"Tony," she said nervously, "won't you do it now? It won't take long, and it will be better for you when you go— Oh, Tony, don't—don't laugh. Please, Tony, here's the priest."

But the Titan roared aloud: "No; get out. Think I'm a-going to give you a chance to grab my money now? Let me die and go to hell in peace."

Father Leblanc knelt meekly and prayed, and the woman's weak pleadings continued,—

"Tony, I've been true and good and faithful to you. Don't die and leave me no better than before. Tony, I do want to be a good woman once, a real-for-true married woman. Tony, here's the priest; say yes." And she wrung her ringless hands.

"You want my money," said Tony, slowly, "and you sha'n't have it, not a cent; John shall have it."

Father Leblanc shrank away like a fading spectre. He came next day and next day, only to see re-enacted the same piteous scene,—the woman pleading to be made a wife ere death hushed Tony's blasphemies, the man chuckling in pain-racked glee at the prospect of her bereaved misery. Not all the prayers of Father Leblanc nor the wailings of Mrs. Murphy could alter the determination of the will beneath the shock of hair; he gloated in his physical weakness at the tenacious grasp on his mentality.

"Tony," she wailed on the last day, her voice rising to a shriek in its eagerness, "tell them I'm your wife; it'll be the same. Only say it, Tony, before you die!"

He raised his head, and turned stiff eyes and gibbering mouth on her; then, with one chill finger pointing at John, fell back dully and heavily.

They buried him with many honours by the Society of Italia's Sons. John took possession of the shop when they returned home, and found the money hidden in the chimney corner.

As for Tony's wife, since she was not his wife after all, they sent her forth in the world penniless, her worn fingers clutching her bundle of clothes in nervous agitation, as though they regretted the time lost from knitting.

THE FISHERMAN OF PASS CHRISTIAN

The swift breezes on the beach at Pass Christian meet and conflict as though each strove for the mastery of the air. The land-breeze blows down through the pines, resinous, fragrant, cold, bringing breath-like memories of dim, dark woods shaded by myriad pine-needles. The breeze from the Gulf is warm and soft and languorous, blowing up from the south with its suggestion of tropical warmth and passion. It is strong and masterful, and tossed Annette's hair and whipped her skirts about her in bold disregard for the proprieties.

Arm in arm with Philip, she was strolling slowly down the great pier which extends from the Mexican Gulf Hotel into the waters of the Sound. There was no moon to-night, but the sky glittered and scintillated with myriad stars, brighter than you can ever see farther North, and the great waves that the Gulf breeze tossed up in restless profusion gleamed with the white fire of phosphorescent flame. The wet sands on the beach glowed white fire; the posts of the pier where the waves had leapt and left a laughing kiss, the sides of the little boats and fish-cars tugging at their ropes, alike showed white and flaming, as though the sea and all it touched were afire.

Annette and Philip paused midway the pier to watch two fishermen casting their nets. With heads bared to the breeze, they stood in clear silhouette against the white background of sea.

"See how he uses his teeth," almost whispered Annette.

Drawing himself up to his full height, with one end of the huge seine between his teeth, and the cord in his left hand, the taller fisherman of the two paused a half instant, his right arm extended, grasping the folds of the net. There was a swishing rush through the air, and it settled with a sort of sob as it cut the waters and struck a million sparkles of fire from the waves. Then, with backs bending under the strain, the two men swung on the cord, drawing in the net, laden with glittering restless fish, which were unceremoniously dumped on the boards to be put into the fish-car awaiting them.

Philip laughingly picked up a soft, gleaming jelly-fish, and threatened to put it on Annette's neck. She screamed, ran, slipped on the wet boards, and in another instant would have fallen over into the water below. The tall fisherman caught her in his arms and set her on her feet.

"Mademoiselle must be very careful," he said in the softest and most correct French. "The tide is in and the water very rough. It would be very difficult to swim out there to-night."

Annette murmured confused thanks, which were supplemented by Philip's hearty tones. She was silent until they reached the pavilion at the end of the pier. The semi-darkness was unrelieved by lantern or light. The strong wind wafted the strains from a couple of mandolins, a guitar, and a tenor voice stationed in one corner to sundry engrossed couples in sundry other corners. Philip found an untenanted nook and they ensconced themselves therein.

"Do you know there's something mysterious about that fisherman?" said Annette, during a lull in the wind.

"Because he did not let you go over?" inquired Philip.

"No; he spoke correctly, and with the accent that goes only with an excellent education."

Philip shrugged his shoulders. "That's nothing remarkable. If you stay about Pass Christian for any length of time, you'll find more things than perfect French and courtly grace among fishermen to surprise you. These are a wonderful people who live across the Lake."

Annette was lolling in the hammock under the big catalpa-tree some days later, when the gate opened, and Natalie's big sun-bonnet appeared. Natalie herself was discovered blushing in its dainty depths. She was only a little Creole seaside girl, you must know, and very shy of the city demoiselles. Natalie's patois was quite as different from Annette's French as it was from the postmaster's English.

"Mees Annette," she began, peony-hued all over at her own boldness, "we will have one lil' hay-ride this night, and a fish-fry at the end. Will you come?"

Annette sprang to her feet in delight. "Will I come? Certainly. How delightful! You are so good to ask me. What shall—what time—" But Natalie's pink bonnet had fled precipitately down the shaded walk. Annette laughed joyously as Philip lounged down the gallery.

"I frightened the child away," she told him.

You've never been for a hay-ride and fish-fry on the shores of the Mississippi Sound, have you? When the summer boarders and the Northern visitors undertake to give one, it is a comparatively staid affair, where due regard is had for one's wearing apparel, and where there are servants to do the hardest work. Then it isn't enjoyable at all. But when the natives, the boys and girls who live there, make up their minds to have fun, you may depend upon its being just the best kind.

This time there were twenty boys and girls, a mamma or so, several papas, and a grizzled fisherman to restrain the ardor of the amateurs. The cart was vast and solid, and two comfortable, sleepy-looking mules constituted the drawing power. There were also tin horns, some guitars, an accordion, and a quartet of much praised voices. The hay in the bottom of the wagon was freely mixed with pine needles, whose prickiness through your hose was amply compensated for by its delicious fragrance.

After a triumphantly noisy passage down the beach one comes to the stretch of heavy sand that lies between Pass Christian proper and Henderson's Point. This is a hard pull for the mules, and the more ambitious riders get out and walk. Then, after a final strain through the shifting sands, bravo! the shell road is reached, and one goes cheering through the pine-trees to Henderson's Point.

If ever you go to Pass Christian, you must have a fish-fry at Henderson's Point. It is the pine-thicketed, white-beached peninsula jutting out from the land, with one side caressed by the waters of the Sound and the other purred over by the blue waves of the Bay of St. Louis. Here is the beginning of the great three-mile trestle bridge to the town of Bay St. Louis, and to-night from the beach could be seen the lights of the villas glittering across the Bay like myriads of unsleeping eyes.

Here upon a firm stretch of white sand camped the merry-makers. Soon a great fire of driftwood and pine cones tossed its flames defiantly at a radiant moon in the sky, and the fishers were casting their nets in the sea. The more daring of the girls waded bare-legged in the water, holding pine-torches, spearing flounders and peering for soft-shell crabs.

Annette had wandered farther in the shallow water than the rest. Suddenly she stumbled against a stone, the torch dropped and spluttered at her feet. With a little helpless cry she looked at the stretch of unfamiliar beach and water to find herself all alone.

"Pardon me, mademoiselle," said a voice at her elbow; "you are in distress?"

It was her fisherman, and with a scarce conscious sigh of relief, Annette put her hand into the outstretched one at her side.

"I was looking for soft shells," she explained, "and lost the crowd, and now my torch is out."

"Where is the crowd?" There was some amusement in the tone, and Annette glanced up quickly, prepared to be thoroughly indignant at this fisherman who dared make fun at her; but there was such a kindly look about his mouth that she was reassured and said meekly,—

"At Henderson's Point."

"You have wandered a half-mile away," he mused, "and have nothing to show for your pains but very wet skirts. If mademoiselle will permit me, I will take her to her friends, but allow me to suggest that mademoiselle will leave the water and walk on the sands."

"But I am barefoot," wailed Annette, "and I am afraid of the fiddlers."

Fiddler crabs, you know, aren't pleasant things to be dangling around one's bare feet, and they are more numerous than sand fleas down at Henderson's Point.

"True," assented the fisherman; "then we shall have to wade back."

The fishing was over when they rounded the point and came in sight of the cheery bonfire with its Rembrandt-like group, and the air was savoury with the smell of frying fish and crabs. The fisherman was not to be tempted by appeals to stay, but smilingly disappeared down the sands, the red glare of his torch making a glowing track in the water.

"Ah, Mees Annette," whispered Natalie, between mouthfuls of a rich croaker, "you have found a beau in the water."

"And the fisherman of the Pass, too," laughed her cousin Ida.

Annette tossed her head, for Philip had growled audibly.

"Do you know, Philip," cried Annette a few days after, rudely shaking him from his siesta on the gallery,—"do you know that I have found my fisherman's hut?"

"Hum," was the only response.

"Yes, and it's the quaintest, most delightful spot imaginable. Philip, do come with me and see it."

"Hum."

"Oh, Philip, you are so lazy; do come with me."

"Yes, but, my dear Annette," protested Philip, "this is a warm day, and I am tired."

Still, his curiosity being aroused, he went grumbling. It was not a very long drive, back from the beach across the railroad and through the pine forest to the bank of a dark, slow-flowing bayou. The fisherman's hut was small, two-roomed, whitewashed, pine-boarded, with the traditional mud chimney acting as a sort of support to one of its uneven sides. Within was a weird assortment of curios from every uncivilized part of the globe. Also were there fishing-tackle and guns in reckless profusion. The fisherman, in the kitchen of the mud-chimney, was sardonically waging war with a basket of little bayou crabs.

"Entrez, mademoiselle et monsieur," he said pleasantly,

grabbing a vicious crab by its flippers, and smiling at its wild attempts to bite. "You see I am busy, but make yourself at home."

"Well, how on earth—" began Philip.

"Sh—sh—" whispered Annette. "I was driving out in the woods this morning, and stumbled on the hut. He asked me in, but I came right over after you."

The fisherman, having succeeded in getting the last crab in the kettle of boiling water, came forward smiling and began to explain the curios.

"Then you have not always lived at Pass Christian," said Philip.

"Mais non, monsieur, I am spending a summer here."

"And he spends his winters, doubtless, selling fish in the French market," spitefully soliloquised Philip.

The fisherman was looking unutterable things into Annette's eyes, and, it seemed to Philip, taking an unconscionably long time explaining the use of an East Indian stiletto.

"Oh, wouldn't it be delightful!" came from Annette at last.

"What?" asked Philip.

"Why, Monsieur LeConte says he'll take six of us out in his catboat tomorrow for a fishing-trip on the Gulf."

"Hum," drily.

"And I'll get Natalie and her cousins."

"Yes," still more drily.

Annette chattered on, entirely oblivious of the strainedness of the men's adieux, and still chattered as they drove through the pines.

"I did not know that you were going to take fishermen and marchands into the bosom of your social set when you came here," growled Philip, at last.

"But, Cousin Phil, can't you see he is a gentleman? The fact that he makes no excuses or protestations is a proof."

"You are a fool," was the polite response.

Still, at six o'clock next morning, there was a little crowd of seven upon the pier, laughing and chatting at the little "Virginie" dipping her bows in the water and flapping her sails in the brisk wind. Natalie's pink bonnet blushed in the early sunshine, and Natalie's mamma, comely and portly, did chaperonage duty. It was not long before the sails gave swell into the breeze and the little boat scurried to the Sound. Past the lighthouse on its gawky iron stalls, she flew, and now rounded the white sands of Cat Island.

"Bravo, the Gulf!" sang a voice on the lookout. The little boat dipped, halted an instant, then rushed fast into the blue Gulf waters.

"We will anchor here," said the host, "have luncheon, and fish."

Philip could not exactly understand why the fisherman should sit so close to Annette and whisper so much into her ears. He chafed at her acting the part of hostess, and was possessed of a murderous desire to throw the pink sun-bonnet and its owner into the sea, when Natalie whispered audibly to one of her cousins that "Mees Annette act nice wit' her lovare."

The sun was banking up flaming pillars of rose and gold in the west when the little "Virginie" rounded Cat Island on her way home, and the quick Southern twilight was fast dying into darkness when she was tied up to the pier and the merry-makers sprang off with baskets of fish. Annette had distinguished herself by catching one small shark, and had immediately ceased to fish and devoted her attention to her fisherman and his line. Philip had angled fiercely, landing trout, croakers, sheepshead, snappers in bewildering luck. He had broken each hopeless captive's neck savagely, as though they were personal enemies. He did not look happy as they landed, though paeans of praise were being sung in his honour.

As the days passed on, "the fisherman of the Pass" began to dance attendance on Annette. What had seemed a joke became serious. Aunt Nina, urged by Philip, remonstrated, and even the mamma of the pink sunbonnet began to look grave. It was all very well for a city demoiselle to talk with a fisherman and accept favours at his hands, provided that the city demoiselle understood that a vast and bridgeless gulf stretched between her and the fisherman.

But when the demoiselle forgot the gulf and the fisherman refused to recognise it, why, it was time to take matters in hand.

To all of Aunt Nina's remonstrances, Philip's growlings, and the averted glances of her companions, Annette was deaf. "You are narrow-minded," she said laughingly. "I am interested in Monsieur LeConte simply as a study. He is entertaining; he talks well of his travels, and as for refusing to recognise the difference between us, why, he never dreamed of such a thing."

Suddenly a peremptory summons home from Annette's father put an end to the fears of Philip. Annette pouted, but papa must be obeyed. She blamed Philip and Aunt Nina for telling tales, but Aunt Nina was uncommunicative, and Philip too obviously cheerful to derive much satisfaction from.

That night she walked with the fisherman hand in hand on the sands. The wind from the pines bore the scarcely recognisable, subtle freshness of early autumn, and the waters had a hint of dying summer in their sob on the beach.

"You will remember," said the fisherman, "that I have told you nothing about myself."

"Yes," murmured Annette.

"And you will keep your promises to me?"

"Yes."

"Let me hear you repeat them again."

"I promise you that I will not forget you. I promise you that I will never speak of you to anyone until I see you again. I promise that I will then clasp your hand wherever you may be."

"And mademoiselle will not be discouraged, but will continue her studies?"

"Yes."

It was all very romantic, by the waves of the Sound, under a harvest moon, that seemed all sympathy for these two, despite the fact that it was probably looking down upon hundreds of other equally romantic couples. Annette went to bed with glowing cheeks, and a heart whose pulsations would have caused a physician to prescribe unlimited digitalis.

It was still hot in New Orleans when she returned home, and it seemed hard to go immediately to work. But if one is going to be an opera-singer some day and capture the world with one's voice, there is nothing to do but to study, study, sing, practise, even though one's throat be parched, one's head a great ache, and one's heart a nest of discouragement and sadness at what seems the uselessness of it all. Annette had now a new incentive to work; the fisherman had once praised her voice when she hummed a barcarole on the sands, and he had insisted that there was power in its rich notes. Though the fisherman had showed no cause why he should be accepted as a musical critic, Annette had somehow respected his judgment and been accordingly elated.

———

It was the night of the opening of the opera. There was the usual crush, the glitter and confusing radiance of the brilliant audience. Annette, with papa, Aunt Nina, and Philip, was late reaching her box. The curtain was up, and "La Juive" was pouring forth defiance at her angry persecutors. Annette listened breathlessly. In fancy, she too was ringing her voice out to an applauding house. Her head unconsciously beat time to the music, and one hand half held her cloak from her bare shoulders.

Then Eleazar appeared, and the house rose at the end of his song. Encores it gave, and bravos and cheers. He bowed calmly, swept his eyes over the tiers until they found Annette, where they rested in a half-smile of recognition.

"Philip," gasped Annette, nervously raising her glasses, "my fisherman!"

"Yes, an opera-singer is better than a marchand," drawled Philip.

The curtain fell on the first act. The house was won by the new tenor; it called and recalled him before the curtain. Clearly he had sung his way into the hearts of his audience at once.

"Papa, Aunt Nina," said Annette, "you must come behind the scenes with me. I want you to meet him. He is delightful. You must come."

Philip was bending ostentatiously over the girl in the next box. Papa and Aunt Nina consented to be dragged behind the scenes. Annette was well known, for, in hopes of some day being an occupant of one of the dressing-rooms, she had made friends with everyone connected with the opera.

Eleazar received them, still wearing his brown garb and patriarchal beard.

"How you deceived me!" she laughed, when the greetings and introductions were over.

"I came to America early," he smiled back at her, "and thought I'd try a little incognito at the Pass. I was not well, you see. It has been of great benefit to me."

"I kept my promise," she said in a lower tone.

"Thank you; that also has helped me."

Annette's teacher began to note a wonderful improvement in his pupil's voice. Never did a girl study so hard or practise so faithfully. It was truly wonderful. Now and then Annette would say to papa as if to reassure herself,—

"And when Monsieur Cherbart says I am ready to go to Paris, I may go, papa?"

And papa would say a "Certainly" that would send her back to the piano with renewed ardour.

As for Monsieur LeConte, he was the idol of New Orleans. Seldom had there been a tenor who had sung himself so completely into the very hearts of a populace. When he was billed, the opera displayed "Standing Room" signs, no matter what the other attractions in the city might be. Sometimes Monsieur LeConte delighted small audiences in Annette's parlour, when the hostess was in a perfect flutter of happiness. Not often, you know, for the leading tenor was in great demand at the homes of society queens.

"Do you know," said Annette, petulantly, one evening, "I wish for the old days at Pass Christian."

"So do I," he answered tenderly; "will you repeat them with me next summer?"

"If I only could!" she gasped.

Still she might have been happy, had it not been for Madame Dubeau,—Madame Dubeau, the flute-voiced leading soprano, who wore the single dainty curl on her forehead, and thrilled her audiences oftentimes more completely than the fisherman. Madame Dubeau was La Juive to his Eleazar, Leonore to his Manfred, Elsa to his Lohengrin, Aida to his Rhadames, Marguerite to his Faust; in brief, Madame Dubeau was his opposite. She caressed him as Mignon, pleaded with him as Michaela, died for him in "Les Huguenots," broke her heart for love of him in "La Favorite." How could he help but love her, Annette asked herself, how could he? Madame Dubeau was beautiful and gifted and charming.

Once she whispered her fears to him when there was the meagrest bit of an opportunity. He laughed. "You don't understand, little one," he said tenderly; "the relations of professional people to each other are peculiar. After you go to Paris, you will know."

Still, New Orleans had built up its romance, and gossiped accordingly.

"Have you heard the news?" whispered Lola to Annette, leaning from her box at the opera one night. The curtain had just gone up on "Herodias," and for some reason or other, the audience applauded with more warmth than usual. There was a noticeable number of good-humoured, benignant smiles on the faces of the applauders.

"No," answered Annette, breathlessly,—"no, indeed, Lola; I am going to Paris next week. I am so delighted I can't stop to think."

"Yes, that is excellent," said Lola, "but all New Orleans is smiling at the romance. Monsieur LeConte and Madame Dubeau were quietly married last night, but it leaked out this afternoon. See all the applause she's receiving!"

Annette leaned back in her chair, very white and still. Her box was empty after the first act, and a quiet little tired voice that was almost too faint to be heard in the carriage on the way home, said—

"Papa, I don't think I care to go to Paris, after all."

M'SIEU FORTIER'S VIOLIN

Slowly, one by one, the lights in the French Opera go out, until there is but a single glimmer of pale yellow flickering in the great dark space, a few moments ago all a-glitter with jewels and the radiance of womanhood and a-clash with music. Darkness now, and silence, and a great haunted hush over all, save for the distant cheery voice of a stage hand humming a bar of the opera.

The glimmer of gas makes a halo about the bowed white head of a little old man putting his violin carefully away in its case with aged, trembling, nervous fingers. Old M'sieu Fortier was the last one out every night.

Outside the air was murky, foggy. Gas and electricity were but faint splotches of light on the thick curtain of fog and mist. Around the opera was a mighty bustle of carriages and drivers and footmen, with a car gaining headway in the street now and then, a howling of names and numbers, the laughter and small talk of cloaked society stepping slowly to its carriages, and the more bourgeoisie vocalisation of the foot passengers who streamed along and hummed little bits of music. The fog's denseness was confusing, too, and at one moment it seemed that the little narrow street would become inextricably choked and remain so until some mighty engine would blow the crowd into atoms. It had been a crowded night. From around Toulouse Street, where led the entrance to the troisièmes, from the grand stairway, from the entrance to the quatrièmes, the human stream poured into the street, nearly all with a song on their lips.

M'sieu Fortier stood at the corner, blinking at the beautiful ladies in their carriages. He exchanged a hearty salutation with the saloon-keeper at the corner, then, tenderly carrying his violin case, he trudged down Bourbon Street, a little old, bent, withered figure, with shoulders shrugged up to keep warm, as though the faded brown overcoat were not thick enough.

Down on Bayou Road, not so far from Claiborne Street, was a house, little and old and queer, but quite large enough to hold M'sieu Fortier, a wrinkled dame, and a white cat. He was home but little, for on nearly every day there were rehearsals; then on Tuesday, Thursday, and Saturday nights, and twice Sundays there were performances, so Ma'am Jeanne and the white cat kept house almost always alone. Then, when M'sieu Fortier was at home, why, it was practice, practice all the day, and smoke, snore, sleep at night. Altogether it was not very exhilarating.

M'sieu Fortier had played first violin in the orchestra ever since—well, no one remembered his not playing there. Sometimes there would come breaks in the seasons, and for a year the great building would be dark and silent. Then M'sieu Fortier would do jobs of playing here and there, one night for this ball, another night for that soirée dansante, and in the day, work at his trade,—that of a cigar-maker. But now for seven years there had been no break in the season, and the little old violinist was happy. There is nothing sweeter than a regular job and good music to play, music into which one can put some soul, some expression, and which one must study to understand. Dance music, of the frivolous, frothy kind deemed essential to soirées, is trivial, easy, uninteresting.

So M'sieu Fortier, Ma'am Jeanne, and the white cat lived a peaceful, uneventful existence out on Bayou Road. When the opera season was over in February, M'sieu went back to cigar-making, and the white cat purred none the less contentedly.

It had been a benefit to-night for the leading tenor, and he had chosen "Roland à Ronceveaux," a favourite this season, for his farewell. And, mon Dieu, mused the little M'sieu, but how his voice had rung out bell-like, piercing above the chorus of the first act! Encore after encore was given, and the bravos of the troisièmes were enough to stir the most sluggish of pulses.

> *"Superbes Pyrenées*
> *Qui dressez dans le ciel,*
> *Vos cimes couronnées*
> *D'un hiver éternelle,*
> *Pour nous livrer passage*
> *Ouvrez vos larges flancs,*
> *Faîtes faire l'orage,*
> *Voici, venir les Francs!"*

M'sieu quickened his pace down Bourbon Street as he sang the chorus to himself in a thin old voice, and then, before he could see in the thick fog, he had run into two young men.

"I—I—beg your pardon,—messieurs," he stammered.

"Most certainly," was the careless response; then the speaker, taking a second glance at the object of the rencontre, cried joyfully:

"Oh, M'sieu Fortier, is it you? Why, you are so happy,

singing your love sonnet to your lady's eyebrow, that you didn't see a thing but the moon, did you? And who is the fair one who should clog your senses so?"

There was a deprecating shrug from the little man.

"Ma foi, but monsieur must know fo' sho', dat I am too old for love songs!"

"I know nothing save that I want that violin of yours. When is it to be mine, M'sieu Fortier?"

"Nevare, nevare!" exclaimed M'sieu, gripping on as tightly to the case as if he feared it might be wrenched from him. "Me a lovere, and to sell mon violon! Ah, so ver' foolish!"

"Martel," said the first speaker to his companion as they moved on up town, "I wish you knew that little Frenchman. He's a unique specimen. He has the most exquisite violin I've seen in years; beautiful and mellow as a genuine Cremona, and he can make the music leap, sing, laugh, sob, skip, wail, anything you like from under his bow when he wishes. It's something wonderful. We are good friends. Picked him up in my French-town rambles. I've been trying to buy that instrument since—"

"To throw it aside a week later?" lazily inquired Martel. "You are like the rest of these nineteenth-century vandals, you can see nothing picturesque that you do not wish to deface for a souvenir; you cannot even let simple happiness alone, but must needs destroy it in a vain attempt to make it your own or parade it as an advertisement."

As for M'sieu Fortier, he went right on with his song and turned into Bayou Road, his shoulders still shrugged high as though he were cold, and into the quaint little house, where Ma'am Jeanne and the white cat, who always waited up for him at nights, were both nodding over the fire.

It was not long after this that the opera closed, and M'sieu went back to his old out-of-season job. But somehow he did not do as well this spring and summer as always. There is a certain amount of cunning and finesse required to roll a cigar just so, that M'sieu seemed to be losing, whether from age or deterioration it was hard to tell. Nevertheless, there was just about half as much money coming in as formerly, and the quaint little pucker between M'sieu's eyebrows which served for a frown came oftener and stayed longer than ever before.

"Minesse," he said one day to the white cat,—he told all his troubles to her; it was of no use to talk to Ma'am Jeanne, she was too deaf to understand,—"Minesse, we are gettin' po'. You' père git h'old, an' hees han's dey go no mo' rapidement, an' dere be no mo' soirées dese day. Minesse, eef la saison don' hurry up, we shall eat ver' lil' meat."

And Minesse curled her tail and purred.

Before the summer had fairly begun, strange rumours began to float about in musical circles. M. Maugé would no longer manage the opera, but it would be turned into the hands of Americans, a syndicate. Bah! These English-speaking people could do nothing unless there was a trust, a syndicate, a company immense and dishonest. It was going to be a guarantee business, with a strictly financial basis. But worse than all this, the new manager, who was now in France, would not only procure the artists, but a new orchestra, a new leader. M'sieu Fortier grew apprehensive at this, for he knew what the loss of his place would mean to him.

September and October came, and the papers were filled with accounts of the new artists from France and of the new orchestra leader too. He was described as a most talented, progressive, energetic young man. M'sieu Fortier's heart sank at the word "progressive." He was anything but that. The New Orleans Creole blood flowed too sluggishly in his old veins.

November came; the opera reopened. M'sieu Fortier was not re-engaged.

"Minesse," he said with a catch in his voice that strongly resembled a sob, "Minesse, we mus' go hongry sometime. Ah, mon pauvre violon! Ah, mon Dieu, dey put us h'out, an' dey will not have us. Nev' min', we will sing anyhow." And drawing his bow across the strings, he sang in his thin, quavering voice, "Salut demeure, chaste et pure."

It is strange what a peculiar power of fascination former haunts have for the human mind. The criminal, after he has fled from justice, steals back and skulks about the scene of his crime; the employee thrown from work hangs about the place of his former industry; the schoolboy, truant or expelled, peeps in at the school-gate and taunts the good boys within. M'sieu Fortier was no exception. Night after night of the performances he climbed the stairs of the opera and sat, an attentive listener to the orchestra, with one ear inclined to the stage, and a quizzical expression on his wrinkled face. Then he would go home, and pat Minesse, and fondle the violin.

"Ah, Minesse, dose new player! Not one bit can dey play. Such tones, Minesse, such tones! All the time portemento, oh, so ver' bad! Ah, mon chere violon, we can play." And he would play and sing a romance, and smile tenderly to himself.

At first it used to be into the deuxièmes that M'sieu Fortier went, into the front seats. But soon they were too expensive, and after all, one could hear just as well in the fourth row as in the first. After a while even the rear row of the deuxièmes was too costly, and the little musician wended his way with the plebeians around on Toulouse Street, and climbed the long, tedious flight of stairs into the troisièmes. It makes no difference to be one row higher. It was more to the liking, after all. One felt more at home up here among the people. If one was thirsty, one could drink a glass of wine or beer being passed about by the libretto boys, and the music sounded just as well.

But it happened one night that M'sieu could not even afford to climb the Toulouse Street stairs. To be sure, there was yet another gallery, the quatrièmes, where the peanut boys went for a dime, but M'sieu could not get down to that yet. So he stayed outside until all the beautiful women in their warm wraps, a bright-hued chattering throng, came down the grand staircase to their carriages.

It was on one of these nights that Courcey and Martel found him shivering at the corner.

"Hello, M'sieu Fortier," cried Courcey, "are you ready to let me have that violin yet?"

"For shame!" interrupted Martel.

"Fifty dollars, you know," continued Courcey, taking no heed of his friend's interpolation.

M'sieu Fortier made a courtly bow. "Eef Monsieur will call at my 'ouse on de morrow, he may have mon violon," he said huskily; then turned abruptly on his heel, and went down Bourbon Street, his shoulders drawn high as though he were cold.

When Courcey and Martel entered the gate of the little house on Bayou Road the next day, there floated out to their ears a wordless song thrilling from the violin, a song that told more than speech or tears or gestures could have done of the utter sorrow and desolation of the little old man. They walked softly up the short red brick walk and tapped at the door. Within, M'sieu Fortier was caressing the violin, with silent tears streaming down his wrinkled gray face.

There was not much said on either side. Courcey came away with the instrument, leaving the money behind, while

Martel grumbled at the essentially sordid, mercenary spirit of the world. M'sieu Fortier turned back into the room, after bowing his visitors out with old-time French courtliness, and turning to the sleepy white cat, said with a dry sob:

"Minesse, dere's only me an' you now."

About six days later, Courcey's morning dreams were disturbed by the announcement of a visitor. Hastily doing a toilet, he descended the stairs to find M'sieu Fortier nervously pacing the hall floor.

"I come fo' bring back you' money, yaas. I cannot sleep, I cannot eat, I only cry, and t'ink, and weesh fo' mon violon; and Minesse, an' de ol' woman too, dey mope an' look bad too, all for mon violon. I try fo' to use dat money, but eet burn an' sting lak blood money. I feel lak' I done sol' my child. I cannot go at l'opera no mo', I t'ink of mon violon. I starve befo' I live widout. My heart, he is broke, I die for mon violon."

Courcey left the room and returned with the instrument.

"M'sieu Fortier," he said, bowing low, as he handed the case to the little man, "take your violin; it was a whim with me, a passion with you. And as for the money, why, keep that too; it was worth a hundred dollars to have possessed such an instrument even for six days."

BY THE BAYOU ST. JOHN

The Bayou St. John slowly makes its dark-hued way through reeds and rushes, high banks and flat slopes, until it casts itself into the turbulent bosom of Lake Pontchartrain. It is dark, like the passionate women of Egypt; placid, like their broad brows; deep, silent, like their souls. Within its bosom are hidden romances and stories, such as were sung by minstrels of old. From the source to the mouth is not far distant, visibly speaking, but in the life of the bayou a hundred heart-miles could scarce measure it. Just where it winds about the northwest of the city are some of its most beautiful bits, orange groves on one side, and quaint old Spanish gardens on the other. Who cares that the bridges are modern, and that here and there pert boat-houses rear their prim heads? It is the bayou, even though it be invaded with the ruthless vandalism of the improving idea, and can a boat-house kill the beauty of a moss-grown centurion of an oak with a history as old as the city? Can an iron bridge with tarantula piers detract from the song of a mocking-bird in a fragrant orange grove? We know that farther out, past the Confederate Soldiers' Home,—that rose-embowered, rambling place of gray-coated, white-haired old men with broken hearts for a lost cause,—it flows, unimpeded by the faintest conception of man, and we love it all the more that, like the Priestess of Isis, it is calm-browed, even in indignity.

To its banks at the end of Moss Street, one day there came a man and a maiden. They were both tall and lithe and slender, with the agility of youth and fire. He was the final concentration of the essence of Spanish passion filtered into an American frame; she, a repressed Southern exotic, trying to fit itself into the niches of a modern civilisation. Truly, a fitting couple to seek the bayou banks.

They climbed the levee that stretched a feeble check to waters that seldom rise, and on the other side of the embankment, at the brink of the river, she sat on a log, and impatiently pulled off the little cap she wore. The skies were gray, heavy, overcast, with an occasional wind-rift in the clouds that only revealed new depths of grayness behind; the tideless waters murmured a faint ripple against the logs and jutting beams of the breakwater, and were answered by the crescendo wail of the dried reeds on the other bank,—reeds that rustled and moaned among themselves for the golden days of summer sunshine.

He stood up, his dark form a slender silhouette against the sky; she looked upward from her log, and their eyes met with an exquisite shock of recognising understanding; dark eyes into dark eyes, Iberian fire into Iberian fire, soul unto soul: it was enough. He sat down and took her into his arms, and in the eerie murmur of the storm coming they talked of the future.

"And then I hope to go to Italy or France. It is only there, beneath those far Southern skies, that I could ever hope to attain to anything that the soul within me says I can. I have wasted so much time in the mere struggle for bread, while the powers of a higher calling have clamoured for recogni-

tion and expression. I will go some day and redeem myself."

She was silent a moment, watching with half-closed lids a
dejected-looking hunter on the other bank, and a lean dog
who trailed through the reeds behind him with drooping
tail. Then she asked:

"And I—what will become of me?"

"You, Athanasia? There is a great future before you, little
woman, and I and my love can only mar it. Try to forget me
and go your way. I am only the epitome of unhappiness and
ill-success."

But she laughed and would have none of it.

Will you ever forget that day, Athanasia? How the little
gamins, Creole throughout, came half shyly near the log,
fishing, and exchanging furtive whispers and half-concealed
glances at the silent couple. Their angling was rewarded
only by a little black water-moccasin that wriggled and
forked its venomous red tongue in an attempt to exercise its
death-dealing prerogative. This Athanasia insisted must go
back into its native black waters, and paid the price the boys
asked that it might enjoy its freedom. The gamins laughed
and chattered in their soft patois; the Don smiled tenderly
upon Athanasia, and she durst not look at the reeds as she
talked, lest their crescendo sadness yield a foreboding. Just
then a wee girl appeared, clad in a multi-hued garment, evidently a sister to the small fishermen. Her keen black eyes
set in a dusky face glanced sharply and suspiciously at the
group as she clambered over the wet embankment, and it
seemed the drizzling mist grew colder, the sobbing wind
more pronounced in its prophetic wail. Athanasia rose suddenly. "Let us go," she said; "the eternal feminine has spoiled
it all."

—

The bayou flows as calmly, as darkly, as full of hidden passions as ever. On a night years after, the moon was shining upon it with a silvery tenderness that seemed brighter, more caressingly lingering than anywhere within the old city. Behind, there rose the spires and towers; before, only the reeds, green now, and soft in their rustlings and whisperings for the future. False reeds! They tell themselves of their happiness to be, and it all ends in dry stalks and drizzling skies. The mocking-bird in the fragrant orange grove sends out his night song, and blends it with the cricket's chirp, as the blossoms of orange and magnolia mingle their perfume with the earthy smell of a summer rain just blown over. Perfect in its stillness, absolute in its beauty, tenderly healing in its suggestion of peace, the night in its clear-lighted, cloudless sweetness enfolds Athanasia, as she stands on the levee and gazes down at the old log, now almost hidden in the luxuriant grass.

"It was the eternal feminine that spoiled our dream that day as it spoiled the after life, was it not?"

But the Bayou St. John did not answer. It merely gathered into its silent bosom another broken-hearted romance, and flowed dispassionately on its way.

WHEN THE BAYOU OVERFLOWS

When the sun goes down behind the great oaks along the Bayou Teche near Franklin, it throws red needles of light into the dark woods, and leaves a great glow on the still bayou. Ma'am Mouton paused at her gate and cast a contemplative look at the red sky.

"Hit will rain to-morrow, sho'. I mus' git in my t'ings."

Ma'am Mouton's remark must have been addressed to herself or to the lean dog, for no one else was visible. She moved briskly about the yard, taking things from the line, when Louisette's voice called cheerily:

"Ah, Ma'am Mouton, can I help?"

Louisette was petite and plump and black-haired. Louisette's eyes danced, and her lips were red and tempting. Ma'am Mouton's face relaxed as the small brown hands relieved hers of their burden.

"Sylves', has he come yet?" asked the red mouth.

"Mais non, ma chère," said Ma'am Mouton, sadly, "I can' tell fo' w'y he no come home soon dese day. Ah me, I feel lak' somet'ing goin' happen. He so strange."

Even as she spoke a quick nervous step was heard crunching up the brick walk. Sylves' paused an instant without the kitchen door, his face turned to the setting sun. He was tall and slim and agile; a true 'cajan.

"Bon jour, Louisette," he laughed. "Eh, maman!"

"Ah, my son, you are ver' late."

Sylves' frowned, but said nothing. It was a silent supper that followed. Louisette was sad, Ma'am Mouton sighed now and then, Sylves' was constrained.

"Maman," he said at length, "I am goin' away."

Ma'am Mouton dropped her fork and stared at him with unseeing eyes; then, as she comprehended his remark, she put her hand out to him with a pitiful gesture.

"Sylves'!" cried Louisette, springing to her feet.

"Maman, don't, don't!" he said weakly; then gathering strength from the silence, he burst forth:

"Yaas, I 'm goin' away to work. I 'm tired of dis, jus' dig, dig, work in de fiel', nothin' to see but de cloud, de tree, de bayou. I don't lak' New Orleans; it too near here, dere no mo' money dere. I go up fo' Mardi Gras, an' de same people, de same strit'. I'm goin' to Chicago!"

"Sylves'!" screamed both women at once.

Chicago! That vast, far-off city that seemed in another world. Chicago! A name to conjure with for wickedness.

"W'y, yaas," continued Sylves', "lots of boys I know dere. Henri an' Joseph Lascaud an' Arthur, dey write me what money dey mek' in cigar. I can mek' a livin' too. I can mek' fine cigar. See how I do in New Orleans in de winter."

"Oh, Sylves'," wailed Louisette, "den you'll forget me!"

"Non, non, ma chère," he answered tenderly. "I will come back when the bayou overflows again, an' maman an' Louisette will have fine present."

Ma'am Mouton had bowed her head on her hands, and was rocking to and fro in an agony of dry-eyed misery.

Sylves' went to her side and knelt. "Maman," he said softly, "maman, you mus' not cry. All de boys go 'way, an' I will come back reech, an' you won't have fo' to work no mo'."

But Ma'am Mouton was inconsolable.

It was even as Sylves' had said. In the summer-time the boys of the Bayou Teche would work in the field or in the town of Franklin, hack-driving and doing odd jobs. When winter came, there was a general exodus to New Orleans, a hundred miles away, where work was to be had as cigar-makers. There is money, plenty of it, in cigar-making, if one can get in the right place. Of late, however, there had been a general slackness of the trade. Last winter oftentimes Sylves' had walked the streets out of work. Many were the Creole boys who had gone to Chicago to earn a living, for the cigar-making trade flourishes there wonderfully. Friends of Sylves' had gone, and written home glowing accounts of the money to be had almost for the asking. When one's blood leaps for new scenes, new adventures, and one needs money, what is the use of frittering away time alternately between the Bayou Teche and New Orleans? Sylves' had brooded all summer, and now that September had come, he was determined to go.

Louisette, the orphan, the girl-lover, whom everyone in Franklin knew would some day be Ma'am Mouton's daughter-in-law, wept and pleaded in vain. Sylves' kissed her quivering lips.

"Ma chère," he would say, "t'ink, I will bring you one fine diamon' ring, nex' spring, when de bayou overflows again."

Louisette would fain be content with this promise. As for Ma'am Mouton, she seemed to have grown ages older. Her Sylves' was going from her; Sylves', whose trips to New Orleans had been a yearly source of heart-break, was going far away for months to that mistily wicked city, a thousand miles away.

October came, and Sylves' had gone. Ma'am Mouton had kept up bravely until the last, when with one final cry she extended her arms to the pitiless train bearing him north-ward. Then she and Louisette went home drearily, the one leaning upon the other.

Ah, that was a great day when the first letter came from Chicago!

Louisette came running in breathlessly from the post-office, and together they read it again and again. Chicago was such a wonderful city, said Sylves'. Why, it was always like New Orleans at Mardi Gras with the people. He had seen Joseph Lascaud, and he had a place to work promised him. He was well, but he wanted, oh, so much, to see maman and Louisette. But then, he could wait.

Was ever such a wonderful letter? Louisette sat for an hour afterwards building gorgeous air-castles, while Ma'am Mouton fingered the paper and murmured prayers to the Virgin for Sylves'. When the bayou overflowed again? That would be in April. Then Louisette caught herself looking critically at her slender brown fingers, and blushed furiously, though Ma'am Mouton could not see her in the gathering twilight.

Next week there was another letter, even more wonderful than the first. Sylves' had found work. He was making cigars, and was earning two dollars a day. Such wages! Ma'am Mouton and Louisette began to plan pretty things for the brown cottage on the Teche.

That was a pleasant winter, after all. True, there was no Sylves', but then he was always in New Orleans for a few months any way. There were his letters, full of wondrous tales of the great queer city, where cars went by ropes un-derground, and where there was no Mardi Gras and the people did not mind Lent. Now and then there would be a present, a keepsake for Louisette, and some money for maman. They would plan improvements for the cottage, and

Louisette began to do sewing and dainty crochet, which she would hide with a blush if anyone hinted at a trousseau.

It was March now, and Spring-time. The bayou began to sweep down between its banks less sluggishly than before; it was rising, and soon would spread over its tiny levees. The doors could be left open now, though the trees were not yet green; but then down here the trees do not swell and bud slowly and tease you for weeks with promises of greenness. Dear no, they simply look mysterious, and their twigs shake against each other and tell secrets of the leaves that will soon be born. Then one morning you awake, and lo, it is a green world! The boughs have suddenly clothed themselves all in a wondrous garment, and you feel the blood run riot in your veins out of pure sympathy.

One day in March, it was warm and sweet. Underfoot were violets, and wee white star flowers peering through the baby-grass. The sky was blue, with flecks of white clouds reflecting themselves in the brown bayou. Louisette tripped up the red brick walk with the Chicago letter in her hand, and paused a minute at the door to look upon the leaping waters, her eyes dancing.

"I know the bayou must be ready to overflow," went the letter in the carefully phrased French that the brothers taught at the parochial school, "and I am glad, for I want to see the dear maman and my Louisette. I am not so well, and Monsieur le docteur says it is well for me to go to the South again."

Monsieur le docteur! Sylves' not well! The thought struck a chill to the hearts of Ma'am Mouton and Louisette, but not for long. Of course, Sylves' was not well, he needed some of maman's tisanes. Then he was homesick; it was to be expected.

At last the great day came, Sylves' would be home. The brown waters of the bayou had spread until they were seemingly trying to rival the Mississippi in width. The little house was scrubbed and cleaned until it shone again. Louisette had looked her dainty little dress over and over to be sure that there was not a flaw to be found wherein Sylves' could compare her unfavourably to the stylish Chicago girls.

The train rumbled in on the platform, and two pair of eyes opened wide for the first glimpse of Sylves'. The porter, all officiousness and brass buttons, bustled up to Ma'am Mouton.

"This is Mrs. Mouton?" he inquired deferentially.

Ma'am Mouton nodded, her heart sinking. "Where is Sylves'?"

"He is here, madam."

There appeared Joseph Lascaud, then some men bearing Something. Louisette put her hands up to her eyes to hide the sight, but Ma'am Mouton was rigid.

"It was too cold for him," Joseph was saying to almost deaf ears, "and he took the consumption. He thought he could get well when he come home. He talk all the way down about the bayou, and about you and Louisette. Just three hours ago he had a bad hemorrhage, and he died from weakness. Just three hours ago. He said he wanted to get home and give Louisette her diamond ring, when the bayou overflowed."

MR. BAPTISTE

He might have had another name; we never knew. Some one had christened him Mr. Baptiste long ago in the dim past, and it sufficed. No one had ever been known who had the temerity to ask him for another cognomen, for though he was a mild-mannered little man, he had an uncomfortable way of shutting up oyster-wise and looking disagreeable when approached concerning his personal history.

He was small: most Creole men are small when they are old. It is strange, but a fact. It must be that age withers them sooner and more effectually than those of un-Latinised extraction. Mr. Baptiste was, furthermore, very much wrinkled and lame. Like the Son of Man, he had nowhere to lay his head, save when some kindly family made room for him in a garret or a barn. He subsisted by doing odd jobs, whitewashing, cleaning yards, doing errands, and the like.

The little old man was a frequenter of the levee. Never a day passed that his quaint little figure was not seen moving up and down about the ships. Chiefly did he haunt the Texas and Pacific warehouses and the landing-place of the Morgan-line steamships. This seemed like madness, for these spots are almost the busiest on the levee, and the rough seamen and 'longshoremen have least time to be bothered with small weak folks. Still there was method in the madness of

Mr. Baptiste. The Morgan steamships, as every one knows, ply between New Orleans and Central and South American ports, doing the major part of the fruit trade; and many were the baskets of forgotten fruit that Mr. Baptiste took away with him unmolested. Sometimes, you know, bananas and mangoes and oranges and citrons will half spoil, particularly if it has been a bad voyage over the stormy Gulf, and the officers of the ships will give away stacks of fruit, too good to go into the river, too bad to sell to the fruit-dealers.

You could see Mr. Baptiste trudging up the street with his quaint one-sided walk, bearing his dilapidated basket on one shoulder, a nondescript head-cover pulled over his eyes, whistling cheerily. Then he would slip in at the back door of one of his clients with a brisk,—

"Ah, bonjour, madame. Now here ees jus' a lil' bit fruit, some bananas. Perhaps madame would cook some for Mr. Baptiste?"

And madame, who understood and knew his ways, would fry him some of the bananas, and set it before him, a tempting dish, with a bit of madame's bread and meat and coffee thrown in for lagniappe; and Mr. Baptiste would depart, filled and contented, leaving the load of fruit behind as madame's pay. Thus did he eat, and his clients were many, and never too tired or too cross to cook his meals and get their pay in baskets of fruit.

One day he slipped in at Madame Garcia's kitchen door with such a woe-begone air, and slid a small sack of nearly ripe plantains on the table with such a misery-laden sigh, that madame, who was fat and excitable, threw up both hands and cried out:

"Mon Dieu, Mistare Baptiste, fo' w'y you look lak dat? What ees de mattare?"

For answer, Mr. Baptiste shook his head gloomily and

sighed again. Madame Garcia moved heavily about the kitchen, putting the plantains in a cool spot and punctuating her foot-steps with sundry "Mon Dieux" and "Misères."

"Dose cotton!" ejaculated Mr. Baptiste, at last.

"Ah, mon Dieu!" groaned Madame Garcia, rolling her eyes heavenwards.

"Hit will drive de fruit away!" he continued.

"Misère!" said Madame Garcia.

"Hit will."

"Oui, oui," said Madame Garcia. She had carefully inspected the plantains, and seeing that they were good and wholesome, was inclined to agree with anything Mr. Baptiste said.

He grew excited. "Yaas, dose cotton-yardmans, dose 'longsho'mans, dey go out on one strik'. Dey t'row down dey tool an' say dey work no mo' wid niggers. Les veseaux, dey lay in de river, no work, no cargo, yaas. Den de fruit ship, dey can' mak' lan', de mans, dey t'reaten an' say t'ings. Dey mak' big fight, yaas. Dere no mo' work on de levee, lak dat. Ever'body jus' walk roun' an' say cuss word, yaas!"

"Oh, mon Dieu, mon Dieu!" groaned Madame Garcia, rocking her guinea-blue-clad self to and fro.

Mr. Baptiste picked up his nondescript head-cover and walked out through the brick-reddened alley, talking excitedly to himself. Madame Garcia called after him to know if he did not want his luncheon, but he shook his head and passed on.

Down on the levee it was even as Mr. Baptiste had said. The 'long-shoremen, the cotton-yardmen, and the stevedores had gone out on a strike. The levee lay hot and unsheltered under the glare of a noonday sun. The turgid Mississippi scarce seemed to flow, but gave forth a brazen gleam from its yellow bosom. Great vessels lay against the wharf, silent and unpopulated. Excited groups of men clustered here and there among bales of uncompressed cotton, lying about in disorderly profusion. Cargoes of molasses and sugar gave out a sticky sweet smell, and now and then the fierce rays of the sun would kindle tiny blazes in the cotton and splinter-mixed dust underfoot.

Mr. Baptiste wandered in and out among the groups of men, exchanging a friendly salutation here and there. He looked the picture of woe-begone misery.

"Hello, Mr. Baptiste," cried a big, brawny Irishman, "sure an' you look, as if you was about to be hanged."

"Ah, mon Dieu," said Mr. Baptiste, "dose fruit ship be ruined fo' dees strik'."

"Damn the fruit!" cheerily replied the Irishman, artistically disposing of a mouthful of tobacco juice. "It ain't the fruit we care about, it's the cotton."

"Hear! hear!" cried a dozen lusty comrades.

Mr. Baptiste shook his head and moved sorrowfully away.

"Hey, by howly St. Patrick, here's that little fruit-eater!" called the centre of another group of strikers perched on cotton-bales.

"Hello! Where—" began a second; but the leader suddenly held up his hand for silence, and the men listened eagerly.

It might not have been a sound, for the levee lay quiet and the mules on the cotton-drays dozed languidly, their ears pitched at varying acute angles. But the practised ears of the men heard a familiar sound stealing up over the heated stillness.

"Oh—ho—ho—humph—humph—humph—ho—ho—ho—oh—o—o—humph!"

Then the faint rattle of chains, and the steady thump of a machine pounding.

If ever you go on the levee you'll know that sound, the rhythmic song of the stevedores heaving cotton-bales, and the steady thump, thump, of the machine compressing them within the hold of the ship.

Finnegan, the leader, who had held up his hand for silence, uttered an oath.

"Scabs! Men, come on!"

There was no need for a further invitation. The men rose in sullen wrath and went down the levee, the crowd gathering in numbers as it passed along. Mr. Baptiste followed in its wake, now and then sighing a mournful protest which was lost in the roar of the men.

"Scabs!" Finnegan had said; and the word was passed along, until it seemed that the half of the second District knew and had risen to investigate.

"Oh—ho—ho—humph—humph—humph—oh—ho—ho—oh—o—o—humph!"

The rhythmic chorus sounded nearer, and the cause manifested itself when the curve of the levee above the French Market was passed. There rose a White Star steamer, insolently settling itself to the water as each consignment of cotton bales was compressed into her hold.

"Niggers!" roared Finnegan wrathily.

"Niggers! niggers! Kill 'em, scabs!" chorused the crowd.

With muscles standing out like cables through their blue cotton shirts, and sweat rolling from glossy black skins, the Negro stevedores were at work steadily labouring at the cotton, with the rhythmic song swinging its cadence in the hot air. The roar of the crowd caused the men to look up with momentary apprehension, but at the over-seer's reassuring word they bent back to work.

Finnegan was a Titan. With livid face and bursting veins he ran into the street facing the French Market, and uprooted a huge block of paving stone. Staggering under its weight, he rushed back to the ship, and with one mighty effort hurled it into the hold.

The delicate poles of the costly machine tottered in the air, then fell forward with a crash as the whole iron framework in the hold collapsed.

"Damn ye," shouted Finnegan, "now yez can pack yer cotton!"

The crowd's cheers at this changed to howls, as the Negroes, infuriated at their loss, for those costly machines belong to the labourers and not to the ship-owners, turned upon the mob and began to throw brickbats, pieces of iron, chunks of wood, anything that came to hand. It was pandemonium turned loose over a turgid stream, with a malarial sun to heat the passions to fever point.

Mr. Baptiste had taken refuge behind a bread-stall on the outside of the market. He had taken off his cap, and was weakly cheering the Negroes on.

"Bravo!" cheered Mr. Baptiste.

"Will yez look at that damned fruit-eatin' Frinchman!" howled McMahon. "Cheerin' the niggers, are you?" and he let fly a brickbat in the direction of the bread-stall.

"Oh, mon Dieu, mon Dieu!" wailed the bread-woman.

Mr. Baptiste lay very still, with a great ugly gash in his wrinkled brown temple. Fishmen and vegetable marchands gathered around him in a quick, sympathetic mass. The individual, the concrete bit of helpless humanity, had more interest for them than the vast, vague fighting mob beyond.

The noon-hour pealed from the brazen throats of many bells, and the numerous hoarse whistles of the steam-boats called the unheeded luncheon-time to the levee workers. The war waged furiously, and groans of the wounded mingled with curses and roars from the combatants.

"Killed instantly," said the surgeon, carefully lifting Mr. Baptiste into the ambulance.

Tramp, tramp, tramp, sounded the militia steadily marching down Decatur Street.

"Whist! do yez hear!" shouted Finnegan; and the conflict had ceased ere the yellow river could reflect the sun from the polished bayonets.

You remember, of course, how long the strike lasted, and how many battles were fought and lives lost before the final adjustment of affairs. It was a fearsome war, and many forgot afterwards whose was the first life lost in the struggle,—poor little Mr. Baptiste's, whose body lay at the Morgue unclaimed for days before it was finally dropped unnamed into Potter's Field.

A CARNIVAL JANGLE

There is a merry jangle of bells in the air, an all-pervading sense of jester's noise, and the flaunting vividness of royal colours. The streets swarm with humanity,—humanity in all shapes, manners, forms, laughing, pushing, jostling, crowding, a mass of men and women and children, as varied and assorted in their several individual peculiarities as ever a crowd that gathered in one locality since the days of Babel.

It is Carnival in New Orleans; a brilliant Tuesday in February, when the very air gives forth an ozone intensely exhilarating, making one long to cut capers. The buildings are a blazing mass of royal purple and golden yellow, national flags, bunting, and decorations that laugh in the glint of the Midas sun. The streets are a crush of jesters and maskers, Jim Crows and clowns, ballet girls and Mephistos, Indians and monkeys; of wild and sudden flashes of music, of glittering pageants and comic ones, of befeathered and belled horses; a dream of colour and melody and fantasy gone wild in an effervescent bubble of beauty that shifts and changes and passes kaleidoscope-like before the bewildered eye.

A bevy of bright-eyed girls and boys of that uncertain age that hovers between childhood and maturity, were moving down Canal Street when there was a sudden jostle with another crowd meeting them. For a minute there was a deafening clamour of shouts and laughter, cracking of the whips, which all maskers carry, a jingle and clatter of carnival bells, and the masked and unmasked extricated themselves and moved from each other's paths. But in the confusion a tall Prince of Darkness had whispered to one of the girls in the unmasked crowd: "You'd better come with us, Flo; you're wasting time in that tame gang. Slip off, they'll never miss you; we'll get you a rig, and show you what life is."

And so it happened, when a half-hour passed, and the bright-eyed bevy missed Flo and couldn't find her, wisely giving up the search at last, she, the quietest and most bashful of the lot, was being initiated into the mysteries of "what life is."

Down Bourbon Street and on Toulouse and St. Peter Streets there are quaint little old-world places where one may be disguised effectually for a tiny consideration. Thither, guided by the shapely Mephisto and guarded by the team of jockeys and ballet girls, tripped Flo. Into one of the lowest-ceiled, dingiest, and most ancient-looking of these shops they stepped.

"A disguise for the demoiselle," announced Mephisto to the woman who met them. She was small and wizened and old, with yellow, flabby jaws, a neck like the throat of an alligator, and straight, white hair that stood from her head uncannily stiff.

"But the demoiselle wishes to appear a boy, un petit garçon?" she inquired, gazing eagerly at Flo's long, slender frame. Her voice was old and thin, like the high quavering of an imperfect tuning-fork, and her eyes were sharp as talons in their grasping glance.

"Mademoiselle does not wish such a costume," gruffly responded Mephisto.

"Ma foi, there is no other," said the ancient, shrugging her shoulders. "But one is left now; mademoiselle would make a fine troubadour."

"Flo," said Mephisto, "it's a dare-devil scheme, try it; no one will ever know it but us, and we'll die before we tell. Besides, we must; it's late, and you couldn't find your crowd."

And that was why you might have seen a Mephisto and a slender troubadour of lovely form, with mandolin flung across his shoulder, followed by a bevy of jockeys and ballet girls, laughing and singing as they swept down Rampart Street.

When the flash and glare and brilliancy of Canal Street have palled upon the tired eye, when it is yet too soon to go home to such a prosaic thing as dinner, and one still wishes for novelty, then it is wise to go into the lower districts. There is fantasy and fancy and grotesqueness run wild in the costuming and the behaviour of the maskers. Such dances and whoops and leaps as these hideous Indians and devils do indulge in; such wild curvetings and long walks! In the open squares, where whole groups do congregate, it is wonderfully amusing. Then, too, there is a ball in every available hall, a delirious ball, where one may dance all day for ten cents; dance and grow mad for joy, and never know who were your companions, and be yourself unknown. And in the exhilaration of the day, one walks miles and miles, and dances and skips, and the fatigue is never felt.

In Washington Square, away down where Royal Street empties its stream of children great and small into the broad channel of Elysian Fields Avenue, there was a perfect Indian pow-wow. With a little imagination one might have willed away the vision of the surrounding houses, and fancied one's self again in the forest, where the natives were holding a sacred riot. The square was filled with spectators, masked and unmasked. It was amusing to watch these mimic Red-men, they seemed so fierce and earnest.

Suddenly one chief touched another on the elbow. "See that Mephisto and troubadour over there?" he whispered huskily.

"Yes; who are they?"

"I don't know the devil," responded the other, quietly, "but I'd know that other form anywhere. It's Leon, see? I know those white hands like a woman's and that restless head. Ha!"

"But there may be a mistake."

"No. I'd know that one anywhere; I feel it is he. I'll pay him now. Ah, sweetheart, you've waited long, but you shall feast now!" He was caressing something long and lithe and glittering beneath his blanket.

In a masked dance it is easy to give a death-blow between the shoulders. Two crowds meet and laugh and shout and mingle almost inextricably, and if a shriek of pain should arise, it is not noticed in the din, and when they part, if one should stagger and fall bleeding to the ground, can any one tell who has given the blow? There is nothing but an unknown stiletto on the ground, the crowd has dispersed, and masks tell no tales anyway. There is murder, but by whom? for what? *Quien sabe?*

And that is how it happened on Carnival night, in the last mad moments of Rex's reign, a broken-hearted mother sat gazing wide-eyed and mute at a horrible something that lay across the bed. Outside the long sweet march music of many bands floated in as if in mockery, and the flash of rockets and Bengal lights illumined the dead, white face of the girl troubadour.

LITTLE MISS SOPHIE

When Miss Sophie knew consciousness again, the long, faint, swelling notes of the organ were dying away in distant echoes through the great arches of the silent church, and she was alone, crouching in a little, forsaken black heap at the altar of the Virgin. The twinkling tapers shone pityingly upon her, the beneficent smile of the white-robed Madonna seemed to whisper comfort. A long gust of chill air swept up the aisles, and Miss Sophie shivered not from cold, but from nervousness.

But darkness was falling, and soon the lights would be lowered, and the great massive doors would be closed; so, gathering her thin little cape about her frail shoulders, Miss Sophie hurried out, and along the brilliant noisy streets home.

It was a wretched, lonely little room, where the cracks let the boisterous wind whistle through, and the smoky, grimy walls looked cheerless and unhomelike. A miserable little room in a miserable little cottage in one of the squalid streets of the Third District that nature and the city fathers seemed to have forgotten.

As bare and comfortless as the room was Miss Sophie's life. She rented these four walls from an unkempt little Creole woman, whose progeny seemed like the promised off-spring of Abraham. She scarcely kept the flickering life in her pale little body by the unceasing toil of a pair of bony hands, stitching, stitching, ceaselessly, wearily, on the bands and pockets of trousers. It was her bread, this monotonous, unending work; and though whole days and nights' constant labour brought but the most meagre recompense, it was her only hope of life.

She sat before the little charcoal brazier and warmed her transparent, needle-pricked fingers, thinking meanwhile of the strange events of the day. She had been up town to carry the great, black bundle of coarse pants and vests to the factory and to receive her small pittance, and on the way home stopped in at the Jesuit Church to say her little prayer at the altar of the calm white Virgin. There had been a wondrous burst of music from the great organ as she knelt there, an overpowering perfume of many flowers, the glittering dazzle of many lights, and the dainty frou-frou made by the silken skirts of wedding guests. So Miss Sophie stayed to the wedding; for what feminine heart, be it ever so old and seared, does not delight in one? And why should not a poor little Creole old maid be interested too?

Then the wedding party had filed in solemnly, to the rolling, swelling tones of the organ. Important-looking groomsmen; dainty, fluffy, white-robed maids; stately, satin-robed, illusion-veiled bride, and happy groom. She leaned forward to catch a better glimpse of their faces. "Ah!"—

Those near the Virgin's altar who heard a faint sigh and rustle on the steps glanced curiously as they saw a slight black-robed figure clutch the railing and lean her head against it. Miss Sophie had fainted.

"I must have been hungry," she mused over the charcoal fire in her little room, "I must have been hungry;" and she smiled a wan smile, and busied herself getting her evening meal of coffee and bread and ham.

If one were given to pity, the first thought that would rush to one's lips at sight of Miss Sophie would have been, "Poor little woman!" She had come among the bareness and sordidness of this neighbourhood five years ago, robed in crape, and crying with great sobs that seemed to shake the vitality out of her. Perfectly silent, too, she was about her former life; but for all that, Michel, the quartee grocer at the corner, and Madame Laurent, who kept the rabbé shop opposite, had fixed it all up between them, of her sad history and past glories. Not that they knew; but then Michel must invent something when the neighbours came to him as their fountain-head of wisdom.

One morning little Miss Sophie opened wide her dingy windows to catch the early freshness of the autumn wind as it whistled through the yellow-leafed trees. It was one of those calm, blue-misted, balmy, November days that New Orleans can have when all the rest of the country is fur-wrapped. Miss Sophie pulled her machine to the window, where the sweet, damp wind could whisk among her black locks.

Whirr, whirr, went the machine, ticking fast and lightly over the belts of the rough jeans pants. Whirr, whirr, yes, and Miss Sophie was actually humming a tune! She felt strangely light to-day.

"Ma foi," muttered Michel, strolling across the street to where Madame Laurent sat sewing behind the counter on blue and brown-checked aprons, "but the little ma'amselle sings. Perhaps she recollects."

"Perhaps," muttered the rabbé woman.

But little Miss Sophie felt restless. A strange impulse seemed drawing her up town, and the machine seemed to run slow, slow, before it would stitch all of the endless number of jeans belts. Her fingers trembled with nervous haste as she pinned up the unwieldy black bundle of finished work, and her feet fairly tripped over each other in their eagerness to get to Claiborne Street, where she could board the uptown car. There was a feverish desire to go somewhere, a sense of elation, a foolish happiness that brought a faint echo of colour into her pinched cheeks. She wondered why.

No one noticed her in the car. Passengers on the Claiborne line are too much accustomed to frail little black-robed women with big, black bundles; it is one of the city's most pitiful sights. She leaned her head out of the window to catch a glimpse of the oleanders on Bayou Road, when her attention was caught by a conversation in the car.

"Yes, it's too bad for Neale, and lately married too," said the elder man. "I can't see what he is to do."

Neale! She pricked up her ears. That was the name of the groom in the Jesuit Church.

"How did it happen?" languidly inquired the younger. He was a stranger, evidently; a stranger with a high regard for the faultlessness of male attire.

"Well, the firm failed first; he didn't mind that much, he was so sure of his uncle's inheritance repairing his lost fortunes; but suddenly this difficulty of identification springs up, and he is literally on the verge of ruin."

"Won't some of you fellows who 've known him all your lives do to identify him?"

"Gracious man, we've tried; but the absurd old will expressly stipulates that he shall be known only by a certain quaint Roman ring, and unless he has it, no identification, no fortune. He has given the ring away, and that settles it."

"Well, you 're all chumps. Why doesn't he get the ring from the owner?"

"Easily said; but—it seems that Neale had some little Creole love-affair some years ago, and gave this ring to his dusky-eyed fiancée. You know how Neale is with his love-affairs, went off and forgot the girl in a month. It seems, however, she took it to heart,—so much so that he's ashamed to try to find her or the ring."

Miss Sophie heard no more as she gazed out into the dusty grass. There were tears in her eyes, hot blinding ones that wouldn't drop for pride, but stayed and scalded. She knew the story, with all its embellishment of heartaches. She knew the ring, too. She remembered the day she had kissed and wept and fondled it, until it seemed her heart must burst under its load of grief before she took it to the pawn-broker's that another might be eased before the end came,—that other her father. The little "Creole love affair" of Neale's had not always been poor and old and jaded-looking; but reverses must come, even Neale knew that, so the ring was at the Mont de Piété. Still he must have it, it was his; it would save him from disgrace and suffering and from bringing the white-gowned bride into sorrow. He must have it; but how?

There it was still at the pawn-broker's; no one would have such an odd jewel, and the ticket was home in the bureau drawer. Well, he must have it; she might starve in the attempt. Such a thing as going to him and telling him that he might redeem it was an impossibility. That good, straight-backed, stiff-necked Creole blood would have risen in all its strength and choked her. No; as a present had the quaint Roman circlet been placed upon her finger, as a present should it be returned.

The bumping car rode slowly, and the hot thoughts beat heavily in her poor little head. He must have the ring; but how—the ring—the Roman ring—the white-robed bride starving—she was going mad—ah yes—the church.

There it was, right in the busiest, most bustling part of the town, its fresco and bronze and iron quaintly suggestive of mediaeval times. Within, all was cool and dim and restful, with the faintest whiff of lingering incense rising and pervading the gray arches. Yes, the Virgin would know and have pity; the sweet, white-robed Virgin at the pretty flower-decked altar, or the one away up in the niche, far above the golden dome where the Host was.

Titiche, the busybody of the house, noticed that Miss Sophie's bundle was larger than usual that afternoon. "Ah, poor woman!" sighed Titiche's mother, "she would be rich for Christmas."

The bundle grew larger each day, and Miss Sophie grew smaller. The damp, cold rain and mist closed the white-curtained window, but always there behind the sewing-machine drooped and bobbed the little black-robed figure. Whirr, whirr went the wheels, and the coarse jeans pants piled in great heaps at her side. The Claiborne Street car saw her oftener than before, and the sweet white Virgin in the flowered niche above the gold-domed altar smiled at the little supplicant almost every day.

"Ma foi," said the slatternly landlady to Madame Laurent and Michel one day, "I no see how she live! Eat? Nothin', nothin', almos', and las' night when it was so cold and foggy, eh? I hav' to mek him build fire. She mos' freeze."

Whereupon the rumour spread that Miss Sophie was starving herself to death to get some luckless relative out of jail for Christmas; a rumour which enveloped her scraggy little figure with a kind of halo to the neighbours when she appeared on the streets.

November had merged into December, and the little pile of coins was yet far from the sum needed. Dear God! how the money did have to go! The rent and the groceries and the coal, though, to be sure, she used a precious bit of that. Would all the work and saving and skimping do good? Maybe, yes, maybe by Christmas.

Christmas Eve on Royal Street is no place for a weakling, for the shouts and carousals of the roisterers will strike fear into the bravest ones. Yet amid the cries and yells, the deafening blow of horns and tin whistles, and the really dangerous fusillade of fireworks, a little figure hurried along, one hand clutching tightly the battered hat that the rude merrymakers had torn off, the other grasping under the thin black cape a worn little pocketbook.

Into the Mont de Piété she ran breathless, eager. The ticket? Here, worn, crumpled. The ring? It was not gone? No, thank Heaven! It was a joy well worth her toil, she thought, to have it again.

Had Titiche not been shooting crackers on the banquette instead of peering into the crack, as was his wont, his big, round black eyes would have grown saucer-wide to see little Miss Sophie kiss and fondle a ring, an ugly clumsy band of gold.

"Ah, dear ring," she murmured, "once you were his, and you shall be his again. You shall be on his finger, and perhaps touch his heart. Dear ring, ma chère petite de ma coeur, chérie de ma coeur. Je t'aime, je t'aime, oui, oui. You are his; you were mine once too. To-night, just one night, I'll keep you— then—to-morrow, you shall go where you can save him."

The loud whistles and horns of the little ones rose on the balmy air next morning. No one would doubt it was Christmas Day, even if doors and windows were open wide to let in cool air. Why, there was Christmas even in the very look of the mules on the poky cars; there was Christmas noise in the streets, and Christmas toys and Christmas odours, savoury ones that made the nose wrinkle approvingly, issuing from the kitchen. Michel and Madame Laurent smiled greetings across the street at each other, and the salutation from a passer-by recalled the many-progenied landlady to herself.

"Miss Sophie, well, po' soul, not ver' much Chris'mas for her. Mais, I'll jus' call him in fo' to spen' the day with me. Eet'll cheer her a bit."

It was so clean and orderly within the poor little room. Not a speck of dust or a litter of any kind on the quaint little old-time high bureau, unless you might except a sheet of paper lying loose with something written on it. Titiche had evidently inherited his prying propensities, for the landlady turned it over and read,—

LOUIS,—Here is the ring. I return it to you. I heard you needed it. I hope it comes not too late. SOPHIE.

"The ring, where?" muttered the landlady. There it was, clasped between her fingers on her bosom,—a bosom white and cold, under a cold happy face. Christmas had indeed dawned for Miss Sophie.

SISTER JOSEPHA

Sister Josepha told her beads mechanically, her fingers numb with the accustomed exercise. The little organ creaked a dismal "O Salutaris," and she still knelt on the floor, her white-bonneted head nodding suspiciously. The Mother Superior gave a sharp glance at the tired figure; then, as a sudden lurch forward brought the little sister back to consciousness, Mother's eyes relaxed into a genuine smile.

The bell tolled the end of vespers, and the sombre-robed nuns filed out of the chapel to go about their evening duties. Little Sister Josepha's work was to attend to the household lamps, but there must have been as much oil spilled upon the table to-night as was put in the vessels. The small brown hands trembled so that most of the wicks were trimmed with points at one corner which caused them to smoke that night.

"Oh, cher Seigneur," she sighed, giving an impatient polish to a refractory chimney, "it is wicked and sinful, I know, but I am so tired. I can't be happy and sing any more. It doesn't seem right for le bon Dieu to have me all cooped up here with nothing to see but stray visitors, and always the same old work, teaching those mean little girls to sew, and washing and filling the same old lamps. Pah!" And she polished the chimney with a sudden vigorous jerk which threatened destruction.

They were rebellious prayers that the red mouth murmured that night, and a restless figure that tossed on the hard dormitory bed. Sister Dominica called from her couch to know if Sister Josepha were ill.

"No," was the somewhat short response; then a muttered, "Why can't they let me alone for a minute? That pale-eyed Sister Dominica never sleeps; that's why she is so ugly."

About fifteen years before this night some one had brought to the orphan asylum connected with this convent, du Sacré Coeur, a round, dimpled bit of three-year-old humanity, who regarded the world from a pair of gravely twinkling black eyes, and only took a chubby thumb out of a rosy mouth long enough to answer in monosyllabic French. It was a child without an identity; there was but one name that any one seemed to know, and that, too, was vague,—Camille.

She grew up with the rest of the waifs; scraps of French and American civilization thrown together to develop a seemingly inconsistent miniature world. Mademoiselle Camille was a queen among them, a pretty little tyrant who ruled the children and dominated the more timid sisters in charge.

One day an awakening came. When she was fifteen, and almost fully ripened into a glorious tropical beauty of the type that matures early, some visitors to the convent were fascinated by her and asked the Mother Superior to give the girl into their keeping.

Camille fled like a frightened fawn into the yard, and was only unearthed with some difficulty from behind a group of palms. Sulky and pouting, she was led into the parlour, picking at her blue pinafore like a spoiled infant.

"The lady and gentleman wish you to go home with them, Camille," said the Mother Superior, in the language of the convent. Her voice was kind and gentle apparently; but the child, accustomed to its various inflections, detected a steely ring behind its softness, like the proverbial iron hand in the velvet glove.

"You must understand, madame," continued Mother, in stilted English, "that we never force children from us. We are ever glad to place them in comfortable—how you say that?—quarters—maisons—homes—bien! But we will not make them go if they do not wish."

Camille stole a glance at her would-be guardians, and decided instantly, impulsively, finally. The woman suited her; but the man! It was doubtless intuition of the quick, vivacious sort which belonged to her blood that served her. Untutored in worldly knowledge, she could not divine the meaning of the pronounced leers and admiration of her physical charms which gleamed in the man's face, but she knew it made her feel creepy, and stoutly refused to go.

Next day Camille was summoned from a task to the Mother Superior's parlour. The other girls gazed with envy upon her as she dashed down the courtyard with impetuous movement. Camille, they decided crossly, received too much notice. It was Camille this, Camille that; she was pretty, it was to be expected. Even Father Ray lingered longer in his blessing when his hands pressed her silky black hair.

As she entered the parlour, a strange chill swept over the girl. The room was not an unaccustomed one, for she had swept it many times, but to-day the stiff black chairs, the dismal crucifixes, the gleaming whiteness of the walls, even the cheap lithograph of the Madonna which Camille had always regarded as a perfect specimen of art, seemed cold and mean.

"Camille, ma chère," said Mother, "I am extremely displeased with you. Why did you not wish to go with Monsieur and Madame Lafayé yesterday?"

The girl uncrossed her hands from her bosom, and spread them out in a deprecating gesture.

"Mais, ma mère, I was afraid."

Mother's face grew stern. "No foolishness now," she exclaimed.

"It is not foolishness, ma mère; I could not help it, but that man looked at me so funny, I felt all cold chills down my back. Oh, dear Mother, I love the convent and the sisters so, I just want to stay and be a sister too, may I?"

And thus it was that Camille took the white veil at sixteen years. Now that the period of novitiate was over, it was just beginning to dawn upon her that she had made a mistake.

"Maybe it would have been better had I gone with the funny-looking lady and gentleman," she mused bitterly one night. "Oh, Seigneur, I 'm so tired and impatient; it's so dull here, and, dear God, I 'm so young."

There was no help for it. One must arise in the morning, and help in the refectory with the stupid Sister Francesca, and go about one's duties with a prayerful mien, and not even let a sigh escape when one's head ached with the eternal telling of beads.

A great fête day was coming, and an atmosphere of preparation and mild excitement pervaded the brown walls of the convent like a delicate aroma. The old Cathedral around the corner had stood a hundred years, and all the city was rising to do honour to its age and time-softened beauty. There would be a service, oh, but such a one! with two Cardinals, and Archbishops and Bishops, and all the accompanying glitter of soldiers and orchestras. The little sisters of the Convent du Sacré Coeur clasped their hands in anticipation of the holy joy. Sister Josepha curled her lip, she was so tired of churchly pleasures.

. The day came, a gold and blue spring day, when the air hung heavy with the scent of roses and magnolias, and the sunbeams fairly laughed as they kissed the houses. The old Cathedral stood gray and solemn, and the flowers in Jackson Square smiled cheery birthday greetings across the way. The crowd around the door surged and pressed and pushed in its eagerness to get within. Ribbons stretched across the banquette were of no avail to repress it, and important ushers with cardinal colours could do little more.

The Sacred Heart sisters filed slowly in at the side door, creating a momentary flutter as they paced reverently to their seats, guarding the blue-bonneted orphans. Sister Josepha, determined to see as much of the world as she could, kept her big black eyes opened wide, as the church rapidly filled with the fashionably dressed, perfumed, rustling, and self-conscious throng.

Her heart beat quickly. The rebellious thoughts that will arise in the most philosophical of us surged in her small heavily gowned bosom. For her were the gray things, the neutral tinted skies, the ugly garb, the coarse meats; for them the rainbow, the ethereal airiness of earthly joys, the bonbons and glacés of the world. Sister Josepha did not know that the rainbow is elusive, and its colours but the illumination of tears; she had never been told that earthly ethereality is necessarily ephemeral, nor that bonbons and glacés, whether of the palate or of the soul, nauseate and pall upon the taste. Dear God, forgive her, for she bent with contrite tears over her worn rosary, and glanced no more at the worldly glitter of femininity.

The sunbeams streamed through the high windows in purple and crimson lights upon a veritable fugue of colour. Within the seats, crush upon crush of spring millinery;

within the aisles erect lines of gold-braided, gold-buttoned military. Upon the altar, broad sweeps of golden robes, great dashes of crimson skirts, mitres and gleaming crosses, the soft neutral hue of rich lace vestments; the tender heads of childhood in picturesque attire; the proud, golden magnificence of the domed altar with its weighting mass of lilies and wide-eyed roses, and the long candles that sparkled their yellow star points above the reverent throng within the altar rails.

The soft baritone of the Cardinal intoned a single phrase in the suspended silence. The censer took up the note in its delicate clink clink, as it swung to and fro in the hands of a fair-haired child. Then the organ, pausing an instant in a deep, mellow, long-drawn note, burst suddenly into a magnificent strain, and the choir sang forth, "Kyrie Eleïson, Christe Eleïson." One voice, flute-like, piercing, sweet, rang high over the rest. Sister Josepha heard and trembled, as she buried her face in her hands, and let her tears fall, like other beads, through her rosary.

It was when the final word of the service had been intoned, the last peal of the exit march had died away, that she looked up meekly, to encounter a pair of youthful brown eyes gazing pityingly upon her. That was all she remembered for a moment, that the eyes were youthful and handsome and tender. Later, she saw that they were placed in a rather beautiful boyish face, surmounted by waves of brown hair, curling and soft, and that the head was set on a pair of shoulders decked in military uniform. Then the brown eyes marched away with the rest of the rear guard, and the white-bonneted sisters filed out the side door, through the narrow court, back into the brown convent.

That night Sister Josepha tossed more than usual on her hard bed, and clasped her fingers often in prayer to quell the wickedness in her heart. Turn where she would, pray as she might, there was ever a pair of tender, pitying brown eyes, haunting her persistently. The squeaky organ at vespers intoned the clank of military accoutrements to her ears, the white bonnets of the sisters about her faded into mists of curling brown hair. Briefly, Sister Josepha was in love.

The days went on pretty much as before, save for the one little heart that beat rebelliously now and then, though it tried so hard to be submissive. There was the morning work in the refectory, the stupid little girls to teach sewing, and the insatiable lamps that were so greedy for oil. And always the tender, boyish brown eyes, that looked so sorrowfully at the fragile, beautiful little sister, haunting, following, pleading.

Perchance, had Sister Josepha been in the world, the eyes would have been an incident. But in this home of self-repression and retrospection, it was a life-story. The eyes had gone their way, doubtless forgetting the little sister they pitied; but the little sister?

The days glided into weeks, the weeks into months. Thoughts of escape had come to Sister Josepha, to flee into the world, to merge in the great city where recognition was impossible, and, working her way like the rest of humanity, perchance encounter the eyes again.

It was all planned and ready. She would wait until some morning when the little band of black-robed sisters wended their way to mass at the Cathedral. When it was time to file out the side-door into the courtway, she would linger at prayers, then slip out another door, and unseen glide up Chartres Street to Canal, and once there, mingle in the throng that filled the wide thoroughfare. Beyond this first plan she could think no further. Penniless, garbed, and shaven though she would be, other difficulties never presented themselves to her. She would rely on the mercies of the world to help her escape from this torturing life of inertia. It seemed easy now that the first step of decision had been taken.

The Saturday night before the final day had come, and she lay feverishly nervous in her narrow little bed, wondering with wide-eyed fear at the morrow. Pale-eyed Sister Dominica and Sister Francesca were whispering together in the dark silence, and Sister Josepha's ears pricked up as she heard her name.

"She is not well, poor child," said Francesca. "I fear the life is too confining."

"It is best for her," was the reply. "You know, sister, how hard it would be for her in the world, with no name but Camille, no friends, and her beauty; and then—"

Sister Josepha heard no more, for her heart beating tumultuously in her bosom drowned the rest. Like the rush of the bitter salt tide over a drowning man clinging to a spar, came the complete submerging of her hopes of another life. No name but Camille, that was true; no nationality, for she could never tell from whom or whence she came; no friends, and a beauty that not even an ungainly bonnet and shaven head could hide. In a flash she realised the deception of the life she would lead, and the cruel self-torture of wonder at her own identity. Already, as if in anticipation of the world's questionings, she was asking herself, "Who am I? What am I?"

The next morning the sisters du Sacré Coeur filed into the Cathedral at High Mass, and bent devout knees at the general confession. "Confiteor Deo omnipotenti," murmured the priest; and tremblingly one little sister followed the words, "Je confesse à Dieu, tout puissant—que j'ai beau-

coup péché par pensées—c'est ma faute—c'est ma faute—
c'est ma très grande faute."

The organ pealed forth as mass ended, the throng slowly
filed out, and the sisters paced through the courtway back
into the brown convent walls. One paused at the entrance,
and gazed with swift longing eyes in the direction of narrow,
squalid Chartres Street, then, with a gulping sob, followed
the rest, and vanished behind the heavy door.

THE PRALINE WOMAN

The praline woman sits by the side of the Archbishop's quaint little old chapel on Royal Street, and slowly waves her latanier fan over the pink and brown wares.

"Pralines, pralines. Ah, ma'amzelle, you buy? S'il vous plaît, ma'amzelle, ces pralines, dey be fine, ver' fresh.

"Mais non, maman, you are not sure?

"Sho', chile, ma bébé, ma petite, she put dese up hissef. He's hans' so small, ma'amzelle, lak you's, mais brune. She put dese up dis morn'. You tak' none? No husban' fo' you den!

"Ah, ma petite, you tak'? Cinq sous, bébé, may le bon Dieu keep you good!

"Mais oui, madame, I know you étrangér. You don' look lak dese New Orleans peop'. You lak' dose Yankee dat come down 'fo' de war."

Ding-dong, ding-dong, ding-dong, chimes the Cathedral bell across Jackson Square, and the praline woman crosses herself.

"Hail, Mary, full of grace—

"Pralines, madame? You buy lak' dat? Dix sous, madame, an' one lil' piece fo' lagniappe fo' madame's lil' bébé. Ah, c'est bon!

"Pralines, pralines, so fresh, so fine! M'sieu would lak' some fo' he's lil' gal' at home? Mais non, what's dat you say?

She's daid! Ah, m'sieu, 't is my lil' gal what died long year ago. Misère, misère!

"Here come dat lazy Indien squaw. What she good fo', anyhow? She jes' sit lak dat in de French Market an' sell her filé, an' sleep, sleep, sleep, lak' so in he's blanket. Hey, dere, you, Tonita, how goes you' beezness?

"Pralines, pralines! Holy Father, you give me dat blessin' sho'? Tak' one, I know you lak dat w'ite one. It tas' good, I know, bien.

"Pralines, madame? I lak' you' face. What fo' you wear black? You' lil' boy daid? You tak' one, jes' see how it tas'. I had one lil' boy once, he jes' grow 'twell he's big lak' dis, den one day he tak' sick an' die. Oh, madame, it mos' brek my po' heart. I burn candle in St. Rocque, I say my beads, I sprinkle holy water roun' he's bed; he jes' lay so, he's eyes turn up, he say 'Maman, maman,' den he die! Madame, you tak' one. Non, non, no l'argent, you tak' one fo' my lil' boy's sake.

"Pralines, pralines, m'sieu? Who mak' dese? My lil' gal, Didele, of co'se. Non, non, I don't mak' no mo'. Po' Tante Marie get too ol'. Didele? She's one lil' gal I 'dopt. I see her one day in de strit. He walk so; hit col' she shiver, an' I say, 'Where you gone, lil' gal?' and he can' tell. He jes' crip close to me, an' cry so! Den I tak' her home wid me, and she say he's name Didele. You see dey wa'nt nobody dere. My lil' gal, she's daid of de yellow fever; my lil' boy, he's daid, po' Tante Marie all alone. Didele, she grow fine, she keep house an' mek' pralines. Den, when night come, she sit wid he's guitar an' sing,

"'Tu l'aime ces trois jours,
Tu l'aime ces trois jours,
   Ma coeur à toi,
   Ma coeur à toi,
Tu l'aime ces trois jours!'

"Ah, he's fine gal, is Didele!

"Pralines, pralines! Dat lil' cloud, h'it look lak' rain, I hope no.

"Here come dat lazy I'ishman down de strit. I don't lak' I'ishman, me, non, dey so funny. One day one I'ishman, he say to me, 'Auntie, what fo' you talk so?' and I jes' say back, 'What fo' you say "Faith an' be jabers"?' Non, I don' lak I'ishman, me!

"Here come de rain! Now I got fo' to go. Didele, she be wait fo' me. Down h'it come! H'it fall in de Meesseesip, an' fill up—up—so, clean to de levee, den we have big crivasse, an' po' Tante Marie float away. Bon jour, madame, you come again? Pralines! Pralines!"

ODALIE

Now and then Carnival time comes at the time of the good Saint Valentine, and then sometimes it comes as late as the warm days in March, when spring is indeed upon us, and the greenness of the grass outvies the green in the royal standards.

Days and days before the Carnival proper, New Orleans begins to take on a festive appearance. Here and there the royal flags with their glowing greens and violets and yellows appear, and then, as if by magic, the streets and buildings flame and burst like poppies out of bud, into a glorious refulgence of colour that steeps the senses into a languorous acceptance of warmth and beauty.

On Mardi Gras day, as you know, it is a town gone mad with folly. A huge masked ball emptied into the streets at daylight; a meeting of all nations on common ground, a potpourri of every conceivable human ingredient, but faintly describes it all. There are music and flowers, cries and laughter and song and joyousness, and never an aching heart to show its sorrow or dim the happiness of the streets. A wondrous thing, this Carnival!

But the old cronies down in Frenchtown, who know everything, and can recite you many a story, tell of one sad heart on Mardi Gras years ago. It was a woman's, of course;

for "Il est toujours les femmes qui sont malheureuses," says an old proverb, and perhaps it is right. This woman—a child, she would be called elsewhere, save in this land of tropical growth and precocity—lost her heart to one who never knew, a very common story, by the way, but one which would have been quite distasteful to the haughty judge, her father, had he known.

Odalie was beautiful. Odalie was haughty too, but gracious enough to those who pleased her dainty fancy. In the old French house on Royal Street, with its quaint windows and Spanish courtyard green and cool, and made musical by the plashing of the fountain and the trill of caged birds, lived Odalie in convent-like seclusion. Monsieur le Juge was determined no hawk should break through the cage and steal his dove; and so, though there was no mother, a stern duenna aunt kept faithful watch.

Alas for the precautions of la Tante! Bright eyes that search for other bright eyes in which lurks the spirit of youth and mischief are ever on the look-out, even in church. Dutifully was Odalie marched to the Cathedral every Sunday to mass, and Tante Louise, nodding devoutly over her beads, could not see the blushes and glances full of meaning, a whole code of signals as it were, that passed between Odalie and Pierre, the impecunious young clerk in the courtroom.

Odalie loved, perhaps, because there was not much else to do. When one is shut up in a great French house with a grim sleepy tante and no companions of one's own age, life becomes a dull thing, and one is ready for any new sensation, particularly if in the veins there bounds the tempestuous Spanish-French blood that Monsieur le Juge boasted of. So Odalie hugged the image of her Pierre during the week days, and played tremulous little love-songs to it in the twilight when la Tante dozed over her devotion book, and on

Sundays at mass there were glances and blushes, and may-hap, at some especially remembered time, the touch of finger-tips at the holy-water font, while la Tante dropped her last genuflexion.

Then came the Carnival time, and one little heart beat faster, as the gray house on Royal Street hung out its many-hued flags, and draped its grim front with glowing colours. It was to be a time of joy and relaxation, when every one could go abroad, and in the crowds one could speak to whom one chose. Unconscious plans formulated, and the petite Odalie was quite happy as the time drew near.

"Only think, Tante Louise," she would cry, "what a happy time it is to be!"

But Tante Louise only grumbled, as was her wont.

It was Mardi Gras day at last, and early through her window Odalie could hear the jingle of folly bells on the mask-ers' costumes, the tinkle of music, and the echoing strains of songs. Up to her ears there floated the laughter of the older maskers, and the screams of the little children frightened at their own images under the mask and domino. What a hurry to be out and in the motley merry throng, to be pacing Royal Street to Canal Street, where was life and the world!

They were tired eyes with which Odalie looked at the gay pageant at last, tired with watching throng after throng of maskers, of the unmasked, of peering into the cartsful of singing minstrels, into carriages of revellers, hoping for a glimpse of Pierre the devout. The allegorical carts rumbling by with their important red-clothed horses were beginning to lose charm, the disguises showed tawdry, even the gay-hued flags fluttered sadly to Odalie.

Mardi Gras was a tiresome day, after all, she sighed, and Tante Louise agreed with her for once.

Six o'clock had come, the hour when all masks must be

removed. The long red rays of the setting sun glinted athwart the many-hued costumes of the revellers trooping unmasked homeward to rest for the night's last mad frolic.

Down Toulouse Street there came the merriest throng of all. Young men and women in dainty, fairy-like garb, dancers, and dresses of the picturesque Empire, a butterfly or two and a dame here and there with powdered hair and graces of olden time. Singing with unmasked faces, they danced toward Tante Louise and Odalie. She stood with eyes lustrous and tear-heavy, for there in the front was Pierre, Pierre the faithless, his arms about the slender waist of a butterfly, whose tinselled powdered hair floated across the lace ruffles of his Empire coat.

"Pierre!" cried Odalie, softly. No one heard, for it was a mere faint breath and fell unheeded. Instead the laughing throng pelted her with flowers and candy and went their way, and even Pierre did not see.

You see, when one is shut up in the grim walls of a Royal Street house, with no one but a Tante Louise and a grim judge, how is one to learn that in this world there are faithless ones who may glance tenderly into one's eyes at mass and pass the holy water on caressing fingers without being madly in love? There was no one to tell Odalie, so she sat at home in the dull first days of Lent, and nursed her dear dead love, and mourned as women have done from time immemorial over the faithlessness of man. And when one day she asked that she might go back to the Ursulines' convent where her childish days were spent, only to go this time as a nun, Monsieur le Juge and Tante Louise thought it quite the proper and convenient thing to do; for how were they to know the secret of that Mardi Gras day?

LA JUANITA

If you never lived in Mandeville, you cannot appreciate the thrill of wholesome, satisfied joy which sweeps over its inhabitants every evening at five o'clock. It is the hour for the arrival of the "New Camelia," the happening of the day. As early as four o'clock the trailing smoke across the horizon of the treacherous Lake Pontchartrain appears, and Mandeville knows then that the hour for its siesta has passed, and that it must array itself in its coolest and fluffiest garments, and go down to the pier to meet this sole connection between itself and the outside world; the little, puffy, side-wheel steamer that comes daily from New Orleans and brings the mail and the news.

On this particular day there was an air of suppressed excitement about the little knot of people which gathered on the pier. To be sure, there were no outward signs to show that anything unusual had occurred. The small folks danced with the same glee over the worn boards, and peered down with daring excitement into the perilous depths of the water below. The sun, fast sinking in a gorgeous glow behind the pines of the Tchefuncta region far away, danced his mischievous rays in much the same manner that he did every other day. But there was a something in the air, a something not tangible, but mysterious, subtle. You could catch an indescribable whiff of it in your inner senses, by the half-eager, furtive glances that the small crowd cast at La Juanita.

"Gar, gar, le bateau!" said one dark-tressed mother to the wide-eyed baby. "Et, oui," she added, in an undertone to her companion. "Voilà, La Juanita!"

La Juanita, you must know, was the pride of Mandeville, the adored, the admired of all, with her petite, half-Spanish, half-French beauty. Whether rocking in the shade of the Cherokee-rose-covered gallery of Grandpère Colomés' big house, her fair face bonnet-shaded, her dainty hands gloved to keep the sun from too close an acquaintance, or splashing the spray from the bow of her little pirogue, or fluffing her skirts about her tiny feet on the pier, she was the pet and ward of Mandeville, as it were, La Juanita Alvarez, since Madame Alvarez was a widow, and Grandpère Colomés was strict and stern.

And now La Juanita had set her small foot down with a passionate stamp before Grandpère Colomés' very face, and tossed her black curls about her wilful head, and said she would go to the pier this evening to meet her Mercer. All Mandeville knew this, and cast its furtive glances alternately at La Juanita with two big pink spots in her cheeks, and at the entrance to the pier, expecting Grandpère Colomés and a scene.

The sun cast red glows and violet shadows over the pier, and the pines murmured a soft little vesper hymn among themselves up on the beach, as the "New Camelia" swung herself in, crabby, sidewise, like a fat old gentleman going into a small door. There was the clang of an important bell, the scream of a hoarse little whistle, and Mandeville rushed to the gang-plank to welcome the outside world. Juanita put her hand through a waiting arm, and tripped away with her Mercer, big and blond and brawny. "Un Américain, pah!"

said the little mother of the black eyes. And Mandeville sighed sadly, and shook its head, and was sorry for Grandpère Colomés.

This was Saturday, and the big regatta would be Monday. Ah, that regatta, such a one as Mandeville had never seen! There were to be boats from Madisonville and Amite, from Lewisburg and Covington, and even far-away Nott's Point. There was to be a Class A and Class B and Class C, and the little French girls of the town flaunted their ribbons down the one oak-shaded, lake-kissed street, and dared anyone to say theirs were not the favourite colours.

In Class A was entered, "'La Juanita,' captain Mercer Grangeman, colours pink and gold." Her name, her colours; what impudence!

Of course, not being a Mandevillian, you could not understand the shame of Grandpère Colomés at this. Was it not bad enough for his petite Juanita, his Spanish blossom, his hope of a family that had held itself proudly aloof from "dose Americain" from time immemorial, to have smiled upon this Mercer, this pale-eyed youth? Was it not bad enough for her to demean herself by walking upon the pier with him? But for a boat, his boat, "un bateau Américain," to be named La Juanita! Oh, the shame of it! Grandpère Colomés prayed a devout prayer to the Virgin that "La Juanita" should be capsized.

Monday came, clear and blue and stifling. The waves of hot air danced on the sands and adown the one street merrily. Glassily calm lay the Pontchartrain, heavily still hung the atmosphere. Madame Alvarez cast an inquiring glance toward the sky. Grandpère Colomés chuckled. He had not lived on the shores of the treacherous Lake Pontchartrain for nothing. He knew its every mood, its petulances and passions; he knew this glassy warmth and what it meant. Chuckling again and again, he stepped to the gallery and looked out over the lake, and at the pier, where lay the boats rocking and idly tugging at their moorings. La Juanita in her rose-scented room tied the pink ribbons on her dainty frock, and fastened cloth of gold roses at her lithe waist.

It was said that just before the crack of the pistol La Juanita's tiny hand lay in Mercer's, and that he bent his head, and whispered softly, so that the surrounding crowd could not hear,—

"Juanita mine, if I win, you will?"

"Oui, mon Mercere, eef you win."

In another instant the white wings were off scudding before the rising breeze, dipping their glossy boat-sides into the clear water, straining their cordage in their tense efforts to reach the stake boats. Mandeville indiscriminately distributed itself on piers, large and small, bath-house tops, trees, and craft of all kinds, from pirogue, dory, and pine-raft to pretentious cat-boat and shell-schooner. Mandeville cheered and strained its eyes after all the boats, but chiefly was its attention directed to "La Juanita."

"Ah, voilà, eet is ahead!"

"Mais non, c'est un autre!"

"La Juanita! La Juanita!"

"Regardez Grandpère Colomés!"

Old Colomés on the big pier with Madame Alvarez and his granddaughter was intently straining his weather-beaten face in the direction of Nott's Point, his back resolutely turned upon the scudding white wings. A sudden chuckle of grim satisfaction caused La Petite's head to toss petulantly.

But only for a minute, for Grandpère Colomés' chuckle was followed by a shout of dismay from those whose glance had followed his. You must know that it is around Nott's Point that the storm king shows his wings first, for the little peninsula guards the entrance which leads into the south-east waters of the stormy Rigolets and the blustering Gulf. You would know, if you lived in Mandeville, that when the pines on Nott's Point darken and when the water shows white beyond like the teeth of a hungry wolf, it is time to steer your boat into the mouth of some one of the many calm bayous which flow silently throughout St. Tammany parish into the lake. Small wonder that the cry of dismay went up now, for Nott's Point was black, with a lurid light overhead, and the roar of the grim southeast wind came ominously over the water.

La Juanita clasped her hands and strained her eyes for her namesake. The racers had rounded the second stake-boat, and the course of the triangle headed them directly for the lurid cloud.

You should have seen Grandpère Colomés then. He danced up and down the pier in a perfect frenzy. The thin pale lips of Madame Alvarez moved in a silent prayer; La Juanita stood coldly silent.

And now you could see that the advance guard of the southeast force had struck the little fleet. They dipped and scurried and rocked, and you could see the sails being reefed hurriedly, and almost hear the rigging creak and moan under the strain. Then the wind came up the lake, and struck the town with a tumultuous force. The waters rose and heaved in the long, sullen ground-swell, which betokened serious trouble. There was a rush of lake-craft to shelter. Heavy gray waves boomed against the breakwaters and piers, dashing their brackish spray upon the strained watchers; then with a shriek and a howl the storm burst full, with blinding sheets of rain, and a great hurricane of Gulf wind that threatened to blow the little town away.

La Juanita was proud. When Grandpère and Madame led

her away in the storm, though her face was white, and the rose mouth pressed close, not a word did she say, and her eyes were as bright as ever before. It was foolish to hope that the frail boats could survive such a storm. There was not even the merest excuse for shelter out in the waters, and when Lake Pontchartrain grows angry, it devours without pity.

Your tropical storm is soon over, however, and in an hour the sun struggled through a gray and misty sky, over which the wind was sweeping great clouds. The rain-drops hung diamond-like on the thick foliage, but the long ground-swell still boomed against the breakwaters and showed white teeth, far to the south.

As chickens creep from under shelter after a rain, so the people of Mandeville crept out again on the piers, on the bath-houses, on the breakwater edge, and watched eagerly for the boats. Slowly upon the horizon appeared white sails, and the little craft swung into sight. One, two, three, four, five, six, seven, eight, nine, counted Mandeville. Every one coming in! Bravo! And a great cheer that swept the whole length of the town from the post-office to Black Bayou went up. Bravo! Every boat was coming in. But—was every man?

This was a sobering thought, and in the hush which followed it you could hear the Q. and C. train thundering over the great lake-bridge, miles away.

Well, they came into the pier at last, "La Juanita" in the lead; and as Captain Mercer landed, he was surrounded by a voluble, chattering, anxious throng that loaded him with questions in patois, in broken English, and in French. He was no longer "un Américain" now, he was a hero.

When the other eight boats came in, and Mandeville saw that no one was lost, there was another ringing bravo, and more chattering of questions.

We heard the truth finally. When the storm burst, Captain Mercer suddenly promoted himself to an admiralship and assumed command of his little fleet. He had led them through the teeth of the gale to a small inlet on the coast between Bayou Lacombe and Nott's Point, and there they had waited until the storm passed. Loud were the praises of the other captains for Admiral Mercer, profuse were the thanks of the sisters and sweethearts, as he was carried triumphantly on the shoulders of the sailors adown the wharf to the Maison Colomés.

The crispness had gone from Juanita's pink frock, and the cloth of gold roses were wellnigh petalless, but the hand that she slipped into his was warm and soft, and the eyes that were upturned to Mercer's blue ones were shining with admiring tears. And even Grandpère Colomés, as he brewed on the Cherokee-rose-covered gallery a fiery punch for the heroes, was heard to admit that "some time dose Americain can mos' be lak one Frenchman."

And we danced at the betrothal supper the next week.

TITEE

It was cold that day. The great sharp north-wind swept out Elysian Fields Street in blasts that made men shiver, and bent everything in their track. The skies hung lowering and gloomy; the usually quiet street was more than deserted, it was dismal.

Titee leaned against one of the brown freight cars for protection against the shrill norther, and warmed his little chapped hands at a blaze of chips and dry grass. "Maybe it'll snow," he muttered, casting a glance at the sky that would have done credit to a practised seaman. "Then won't I have fun! Ugh, but the wind blows!"

It was Saturday, or Titee would have been in school, the big yellow school on Marigny Street, where he went every day when its bell boomed nine o'clock, went with a run and a joyous whoop, ostensibly to imbibe knowledge, really to make his teacher's life a burden.

Idle, lazy, dirty, troublesome boy, she called him to herself, as day by day wore on, and Titee improved not, but let his whole class pass him on its way to a higher grade. A practical joke he relished infinitely more than a practical problem, and a good game at pin-sticking was far more entertaining than a language lesson. Moreover, he was always

hungry, and would eat in school before the half-past ten re-
cess, thereby losing much good playtime for his voracious
appetite.

But there was nothing in natural history that Titee did
not know. He could dissect a butterfly or a mosquito hawk,
and describe their parts as accurately as a spectacled student
with a scalpel and microscope could talk about a cadaver.
The entire Third District, with its swamps and canals and
commons and railroad sections, and its wondrous, crooked,
tortuous streets, was an open book to Titee. There was not a
nook or corner that he did not know or could not tell of.
There was not a bit of gossip among the gamins, little Creole
and Spanish fellows, with dark skins and lovely eyes, like
spaniels, that Titee could not tell of. He knew just exactly
when it was time for crawfish to be plentiful down in the
Claiborne and Marigny canals; just when a poor, breadless
fellow might get a job in the big bone-yard and fertilising
factory, out on the railroad track; and as for the levee, with
its ships and schooners and sailors, how he could revel in
them! The wondrous ships, the pretty little schooners, where
the foreign-looking sailors lay on long moonlight nights,
singing to their guitars and telling great stories,—all these
things and more could Titee tell of. He had been down to
the Gulf, and out on its treacherous waters through the Eads
jetties on a fishing-smack with some jolly brown sailors, and
could interest the whole school-room in the talk-lessons, if
he chose.

Titee shivered as the wind swept round the freight-cars.
There isn't much warmth in a bit of a jersey coat.

"Wish 'twas summer," he murmured, casting another sail-
or's glance at the sky. "Don't believe I like snow; it's too wet
and cold." And with a last parting caress at the little fire he

had builded for a minute's warmth, he plunged his hands in his pockets, shut his teeth, and started manfully on his mission out the railroad track toward the swamps.

It was late when Titee came home, to such a home as it was, and he had but illy performed his errand; so his mother beat him and sent him to bed supperless. A sharp strap stings in cold weather, and a long walk in the teeth of a biting wind creates a keen appetite. But if Titee cried himself to sleep that night, he was up bright and early next morning, had been to mass, devoutly kneeling on the cold floor, blowing his fingers to keep them warm, and was home almost before the rest of the family were awake.

There was evidently some great matter of business on the young man's mind, for he scarcely ate his breakfast, and left the table soon, eagerly cramming the remainder of his meal in his pockets.

"Ma foi, but what now?" mused his mother, as she watched his little form sturdily trudging the track in the face of the wind; his head, with the rimless cap thrust close on the shock of black hair, bent low; his hands thrust deep in the bulging pockets.

"A new live play-toy h'it may be," ventured the father; "he is one funny chil."

The next day Titee was late for school. It was something unusual, for he was always the first on hand to fix some plan of mechanism to make the teacher miserable. She looked reprovingly at him this morning, when he came in during arithmetic class, his hair all wind-blown, his cheeks rosy from a hard fight with the sharp blasts. But he made up for his tardiness by his extreme goodness all day; just think, Titee did not even eat once before noon, a something unparalleled in the entire previous history of his school life.

When the lunch-hour came, and all the yard was a scene

of feast and fun, one of the boys found him standing by a post, disconsolately watching a ham sandwich as it rapidly disappeared down the throat of a sturdy, square-headed little fellow.

"Hello, Edgar," he said, "what you got fer lunch?"

"Nothin'," was the mournful reply.

"Ah, why don't you stop eatin' in school, fer a change? You don't ever have nothin' to eat."

"I didn't eat to-day," said Titee, blazing up.

"You did!"

"I tell you I didn't!" and Titee's hard little fist planted a punctuation mark on his comrade's eye.

A fight in the schoolyard! Poor Titee was in disgrace again. Still, in spite of his battered appearance, a severe scolding from the principal, lines to write, and a further punishment from his mother, Titee scarcely remained for his dinner, but was off down the railroad track with his pockets partly stuffed with the remnants of the scanty meal.

And the next day Titee was tardy again, and lunchless too, and the next, until the teacher, in despair, sent a nicely printed note to his mother about him, which might have done some good, had not Titee taken great pains to tear it up on the way home.

One day it rained, whole bucketsful of water, that poured in torrents from a miserable, angry sky. Too wet a day for bits of boys to be trudging to school, so Titee's mother thought; so she kept him at home to watch the weather through the window, fretting and fuming like a regular storm in miniature. As the day wore on, and the rain did not abate, his mother kept a strong watch upon him, for he tried many times to slip away.

Dinner came and went, and the gray soddenness of the skies deepened into the blackness of coming night. Someone called Titee to go to bed, and Titee was nowhere to be found.

Under the beds, in closets and corners, in such impossible places as the soap-dish and water-pitcher even, they searched, but he had gone as completely as if he had been spirited away. It was of no use to call up the neighbors, he had never been near their houses, they affirmed, so there was nothing to do but to go to the railroad track where Titee had been seen so often trudging in the shrill north-wind.

With lanterns and sticks, and his little yellow dog, the rescuing party started down the track. The rain had ceased falling, but the wind blew a gale, scurrying great gray clouds over a fierce sky. It was not exactly dark, though in this part of the city there is neither gas nor electricity, and on such a night as this neither moon nor stars dared show their faces in so gray a sky; but a sort of all-diffused luminosity was in the air, as though the sea of atmosphere was charged with an ethereal phosphorescence.

Search as they did, there were no signs of Titee. The soft earth between the railroad ties crumbled between their feet without showing any small tracks or footprints.

"Mais, we may as well return," said the big brother; "he is not here."

"Oh, mon Dieu," urged the mother, "he is, he is; I know it."

So on they went, slipping on the wet earth, stumbling over the loose rocks, until a sudden wild yelp from Tiger brought them to a standstill. He had rushed ahead of them, and his voice could be heard in the distance, howling piteously.

With a fresh impetus the little muddy party hurried forward. Tiger's yelps could be heard plainer and plainer, mingled now with a muffled, plaintive little wail.

After a while they found a pitiful little heap of sodden rags, lying at the foot of a mound of earth and stones thrown upon the side of the track. It was Titee with a broken leg, all wet and miserable and moaning.

They picked him up tenderly, and started to carry him home. But he cried and clung to the mother, and begged not to go.

"Ah, mon pauvre enfant, he has the fever!" wailed the mother.

"No, no, it's my old man. He's hungry," sobbed Titee, holding out a little package. It was the remnants of his dinner, all wet and rain-washed.

"What old man?" asked the big brother.

"My old man. Oh, please, please don't go home till I see him. I'm not hurting much, I can go."

So, yielding to his whim, they carried him farther away, down the sides of the track up to an embankment or levee by the sides of the Marigny Canal. Then the big brother, suddenly stopping, exclaimed:

"Why, here's a cave. Is it Robinson Crusoe?"

"It's my old man's cave," cried Titee. "Oh, please go in; maybe he's dead."

There cannot be much ceremony in entering a cave. There is but one thing to do,—walk in. This they did, and holding up the lantern, beheld a weird sight. On a bed of straw and paper in one corner lay a withered, wizened, white-bearded old man with wide eyes staring at the unaccustomed light. In the other corner was an equally dilapidated cow.

"It's my old man!" cried Titee, joyfully. "Oh, please, grandpa, I couldn't get here to-day, it rained all mornin' an' when I ran away, I fell down an' broke something, an', oh, grandpa, I'm all tired an' hurty, an' I'm so 'fraid you're hungry."

So the secret of Titee's jaunts down the railroad was out. In one of his trips around the swamp-land, he had discovered the old man exhausted from cold and hunger in the fields. Together they had found this cave, and Titee had gathered the straw and paper that made the bed. Then a tramp cow, old and turned adrift, too, had crept in and shared the damp dwelling. And thither Titee had trudged twice a day, carrying his luncheon in the morning and his dinner in the afternoon.

"There's a crown in heaven for that child," said the officer of charity to whom the case was referred.

But as for Titee, when the leg was well, he went his way as before.

SELECTED STORIES FROM
VIOLETS AND OTHER TALES

VIOLETS

"And she tied a bunch of violets with a tress of her pretty brown hair."

She sat in the yellow glow of the lamplight softly humming these words. It was Easter evening, and the newly risen spring world was slowly sinking to a gentle, rosy, opalescent slumber, sweetly tired of the joy which had pervaded it all day. For in the dawn of the perfect morn, it had arisen, stretched out its arms in glorious happiness to greet the Saviour and said its hallelujahs, merrily trilling out carols of bird, and organ and flower-song. But the evening had come, and rest.

There was a letter lying on the table, it read:

"Dear, I send you this little bunch of flowers as my Easter token. Perhaps you may not be able to read their meaning, so I'll tell you. Violets, you know, are my favorite flowers. Dear, little, human-faced things! They seem always as if about to whisper a love-word; and then they signify that thought which passes always between you and me. The orange blossoms—you know their meaning; the little pinks are the flowers you love; the evergreen leaf is the symbol of the endurance of our affection; the tube-roses I put in, because once when you kissed and pressed me close in your arms, I had a bunch of tube-roses on my bosom, and the heavy fragrance of their crushed loveliness has always lived in my memory. The violets and pinks are from a bunch I wore to-day, and when kneeling at the altar, during communion, did I sin, dear, when I thought of you? The tube-roses and orange-blossoms I wore Friday night; you always wished for a lock of my hair, so I'll tie these flowers with them—but there, it is not stable enough; let me wrap them with a bit of ribbon, pale blue, from that little dress I wore last winter to the dance, when we had such a long, sweet talk in that forgotten nook. You always loved that dress, it fell in such soft ruffles away from the throat and bosom,—you called me your little forget-me-not, that night. I laid the flowers away for awhile in our favorite book,—Byron—just at the poem we loved best, and now I send them to you. Keep them always in remembrance of me, and if aught should occur to separate us, press these flowers to your lips, and I will be with you in spirit, permeating your heart with unutterable love and happiness."

II.

It is Easter again. As of old, the joyous bells clang out the glad news of the resurrection. The giddy, dancing sunbeams laugh riotously in field and street; birds carol their sweet twitterings everywhere, and the heavy perfume of flowers scents the golden atmosphere with inspiring fragrance. One long, golden sunbeam steals silently into the white-curtained window of a quiet room, and lay athwart a sleeping face. Cold, pale, still, its fair, young face pressed against the satin-lined casket. Slender, white fingers, idle now, they that had never known rest; locked softly over a bunch of violets; violets and tube-roses in her soft, brown hair, violets in the bosom of her long, white gown; violets and tube-roses and orange-blossoms banked everywhere, until the air was filled with the ascending souls of the human flowers. Some whispered that a broken heart had ceased to flutter in that still, young form, and that it was a mercy for the soul to ascend on the slender sunbeam. To-day she kneels at the throne of heaven, where one year ago she had communed at an earthly altar.

III.

Far away in a distant city, a man, carelessly looking among some papers, turned over a faded bunch of flowers tied with a blue ribbon and a lock of hair. He paused meditatively awhile, then turning to the regal-looking woman lounging before the fire, he asked:

"Wife, did you ever send me these?"

She raised her great, black eyes to his with a gesture of ineffable disdain, and replied languidly:

"You know very well I can't bear flowers. How could I ever send such sentimental trash to any one? Throw them into the fire."

And the Easter bells chimed a solemn requiem as the flames slowly licked up the faded violets. Was it merely fancy on the wife's part, or did the husband really sigh,— a long, quivering breath of remembrance?

THE WOMAN

The literary manager of the club arose, cleared his throat, adjusted his cravat, fixed his eyes sternly upon the young man, and in a sonorous voice, a little marred by his habitual lisp, asked: "Mr.——, will you please tell us your opinion upon the question, whether woman's chances for matrimony are increased or decreased when she becomes man's equal as a wage earner?"

The secretary adjusted her eye-glass, and held her pencil alertly poised above her book, ready to note which side Mr.—— took. Mr.—— fidgeted, pulled himself together with a violent jerk, and finally spoke his mind. Someone else did likewise, also someone else, then the women interposed, and jumped on the men, the men retaliated, a wordy war ensued, and the whole matter ended by nothing being decided, pro or con—generally the case in wordy discussions. *Moi?* Well, I sawed wood and said nothing, but all the while there was forming in my mind, no, I won't say forming, it was there already. It was this, *Why should well-salaried women marry?* Take the average working-woman of to-day. She works from five to ten hours a day, doing extra night work, sometimes, of course. Her work over, she goes home or to her boarding-house, as the case may be. Her meals are prepared for her, she has no household cares upon her shoulders, no troublesome dinners to prepare for a fault-finding husband, no fretful children to try her patience, no petty bread and meat economies to adjust. She has her cares, her money-troubles, her debts, and her scrimpings, it is true, but they only make her independent, instead of reducing her to a dead level of despair. Her day's work ends at the office, school, factory, or store; the rest of the time is hers, undisturbed by the restless going to and fro of housewifely cares, and she can employ it in mental or social diversions. She does not incessantly rely upon the whims of a cross man to take her to such amusements as she desires. In this nineteenth century she is free to go where she pleases—provided it be in a moral atmosphere—without comment. Theatres, concerts, lectures, and the lighter amusements of social affairs among her associates, are open to her, and there she can go, see, and be seen, admire and be admired, enjoy and be enjoyed, without a single harrowing thought of the baby's milk or the husband's coffee.

Her earnings are her own, indisputably, unreservedly, undividedly. She knows to a certainty just how much she can spend, how well she can dress, how far her earnings will go. If there is a dress, a book, a bit of music, a bunch of flowers, or a bit of furniture that she wants, she can get it, and there is no need of asking anyone's advice, or gently hinting to John that Mrs. So and So has a lovely new hat, and there is one ever so much prettier and cheaper down at Thus & Co.'s. To an independent spirit there is a certain sense of humiliation and wounded pride in asking for money, be it five cents or five hundred dollars. The working woman knows no such pang; she has but to question her account and all is over. In the summer she takes her savings of the winter, packs her trunk and takes a trip more or less extensive, and there is none to say her nay,—nothing to bother her save the accumulation of her own baggage. There is an independent, happy, free-and-easy swing about the motion of her life. Her mind is constantly being broadened by contact with the world in its working clothes; in her leisure moments by the better thoughts of dead and living men which she meets in her applications to books and periodicals; in her vacations, by her studies of nature, or it may be other communities than her own. The freedom which she enjoys she does not trespass upon, for if she did not learn at school she has acquired since habits of strong self-reliance, self-support, earnest thinking, deep discriminations, and firmly believes that the most perfect liberty is that state in which humanity conforms itself to and obeys strictly, without deviation, those laws which are best fitted for their mutual self-advancement.

And so your independent working woman of to day comes as near being ideal in her equable self poise as can be imagined. So why should she hasten to give this liberty up in exchange for a serfdom, sweet sometimes, it is true, but which too often becomes galling and unendurable.

It is not marriage that I decry, for I don't think any really sane person would do this, but it is this wholesale marrying of girls in their teens, this rushing into an unknown plane of life to avoid work. Avoid work! What housewife dares call a moment her own?

Marriages might be made in Heaven, but too often they are consummated right here on earth, based on a desire to possess the physical attractions of the woman by the man, pretty much as a child desires a toy, and an innate love of man, a wild desire not to be ridiculed by the foolish as an "old maid," and a certain delicate shrinking from the work of the world—laziness is a good name for it—by the woman. The attraction of mind to mind, the ability of one to compliment the lights and shadows in the other, the capacity of either to fulfil the duties of wife or husband—these do not enter into the contract. That is why we have divorce courts.

And so our independent woman in every year of her full, rich, well-rounded life, gaining fresh knowledge and experience, learning humanity, and particularly that portion of it which is the other gender, so well as to avoid clay-footed idols, and finally when she does consent to bear the yoke upon her shoulders, does so with perhaps less romance and glamor than her younger scoffing sisters, but with an assurance of solid and more lasting happiness. Why should she have hastened this; was aught lost by the delay?

"They say" that men don't admire this type of woman, that they prefer the soft, dainty, winning, mindless creature who cuddles into men's arms, agrees to everything they say, and looks upon them as a race of gods turned loose upon this earth for the edification of womankind. Well, may be so, but there is one thing positive, they certainly respect the independent one, and admire her, too, even if it is at a distance, and that in itself is something. As to the other part, no matter how sensible a woman is on other questions, when she falls in love she is fool enough to believe her adored one a veritable Solomon. Cuddling? Well, she may preside over conventions, brandish her umbrella at board meetings, tramp the streets soliciting subscriptions, wield the blue pencil in an editorial sanctum, hammer a type-writer, smear her nose with ink from a galley full of pied type, lead infant ideas through the tortuous mazes of c-a-t and r-a-t, plead at the bar, or wield the scalpel in a dissecting room, yet when the right moment comes, she will sink as gracefully into his manly embrace, throw her arms as lovingly around his neck, and cuddle as warmly and sweetly to his bosom as her little sister who has done nothing else but think, dream, and practice for that hour. It comes natural, you see.

ANARCHY ALLEY

To the casual observer, the quaint, narrow, little alley that lies in the heart of the city is no more than any other of the numerous divisions of streets in which New Orleans delights. But to the idle wanderer, or he whose mission down its four squares of much trodden stones is an aimless one,— whose eyes unforced to bend to the ground in thought of sordid ways and means, can peer at will into its quaint corners. Exchange Alley presents all the phases of a Latinized portion of America, a bit of Europe, perhaps, the restless, chafing, anarchistic Europe of to-day, in the midst of the quieter democratic institution of our republic.

It is Bohemia, pure and simple, Bohemia, in all its stages, from the beer saloon and the cheap book-store, to the cheaper cook shop and uncertain lodging house. There the great American institution, the wondrous monarch whom the country supports—the tramp—basks in superior comfort and contented, unmolested indolence. Idleness and labor, poverty and opulence, the honest, law-abiding workingman, and the reckless, restless anarchist, jostle side by side, and brush each other's elbows in terms of equality as they do nowhere else.

On the busiest thoroughfares in the city, just in the busiest part, between two of the most crowded and conservative of cross-streets, lies this alley of Latinism. One might almost pass it hurriedly, avoiding the crowds that cluster at this section of the streets, but upon turning into a narrow section, stone-paved, the place is entered, appearing to end one square distant, seeming to bar itself from the larger buildings by an aimless sort of iron affair, part railing, part posts. There is a conservative book-store at the entrance on one side, and an even more harmless clothing store on the other; then comes a saloon with many blind doors, behind which are vistas of tables, crowded and crowded with men drinking beer out of "globes," large, round, moony, common affairs. There is a dingy, pension-claim office, with cripples and sorrowful-looking women in black, sitting about on rickety chairs. Somehow, there is always an impression with me that the mourning dress and mournful looks are put on to impress the dispenser and adjuster. It is wicked, but what can one do if impressions come?

There are more little cuddies of places, dye-shops, tailors, and nondescript corners that seem to have no possible mission on earth and are sadly conscious of their aimlessness. Then the railing is reached, and the alley instead of ending has merely given itself an angular twist to the right, and extends three squares further, to a great, pale green dome, and stately entrance.

The calmly-thinking, quietly-laboring, cool and conservative world is for the nonce left behind. With the first stepping across Customhouse street, the place widens architecturally, and the atmosphere, too, seems impregnated with a sort of mental freedom, conducive to dangerous theorizing and broody reflections on the inequality of the classes. The sun shines in a strip in the centre, yellow and elusive, like gold; someone is rattling a gay galop on a piano somewhere; there is a sound of mens' voices in a heated discussion, a long whiff of pipe-smoke trails through the sunlight from the bar-room; the clink of glasses, the chink of silver, and the high treble of a woman's voice scolding a refractory child, mingle in incongruous melody.

Two-story houses all along; the first floor divided into cuddies, here a paper store, displaying ten-cent novels of detective stories with impossible cuts, illustrating impossible situations of the plot; dye-shops, jewelers, tailors, tin-smiths, cook-shops, intelligence offices—many of these, and some newspaper offices. On the second floor, balconies, dingy, iron-railed, with sickly box-plants, and decrepit garments airing and being turned and tended by dishevelled, slip-shod women. Lodging-houses these, some of them, but one is forced to wonder why do the tenants sun their clothes so often? The lines stretched from posts to posts seem always filled with airing garments. Is it economy? And do the owners of the faded vests and patched coats hide in dusky corners while their only garments are receiving the benefit of Old Sol's cleansing rays? And are the women with the indiscriminate tresses, near relatives, or only the landladies? It would be something worth knowing if one could.

Plenty of saloons—great, gorgeous, gaudy places, with pianos and swift-footed waiters, tables and cards, and men, men, men. The famous Three Brothers' Saloon occupies a position about midway the alley, and at its doors, the acme, the culminating point, the superlative degree of unquietude and discontent is reached. It is the headquarters of nearly all the great labor organizations in the city. Behind its doors, swinging as easily between the street and the liquor-fumed halls as the soul swings between right and wrong, the disturbed minds of the working-men become clouded, heated, and wrothily ready for deeds of violence.

Outside on the pavements with hundreds of like-excited

men, with angry discussions and bitter recitals of complaints, the seeds of discord sown some time since, perhaps, sprout afresh, blossom and bear fruits. Is there a strike? Then special minions of the law are detailed to this place, for violence and hatred of employers, insurrection and socialism find here ready followers. Impromptu mass meetings are common, and law-breaking schemes find their cradle beneath its glittering lights. It is always thronged within and without, a veritable nursery of riot and disorder.

And oh, Bohemia, pipes, indolence, and beer! The atmosphere is impregnated with it, the dust sifts it into your clothes and hair, the sunlight filters it through your brain, the stray snatches of music now and then beat it rhythmically into your mind. There are some who work, yes, and a few places outside of the saloons that seem to be animated with a business motive. There are even some who push their way briskly through the aimless bodies of men,—but then there must be an occasional anomaly to break the monotony, if nothing more.

It is so unlike the ordinary world, this bit of Bohemia, that one feels a personal grievance when the marble entrance and great, green dome become positive, solid, architectural facts, standing in all the grim solemnity of the main entrance of the Hotel Royal on St. Louis Street, ending, with a sudden return to aristocracy, this stamping ground for anarchy.

A STORY OF VENGEANCE

Yes, Eleanor, I have grown grayer. I am younger than you, you know, but then, what have you to age you? A kind husband, lovely children, while I—I am nothing but a lonely woman. Time goes slowly, slowly for me now.

Why did I never marry? Move that screen a little to one side, please; my eyes can scarcely bear a strong light. Bernard? Oh, that's a long story. I'll tell you if you wish; it might pass an hour.

Do you ever think to go over the old school-days? We thought such foolish things then, didn't we? There wasn't one of us but imagined we would have only to knock ever so faintly on the portals of fame and they would fly wide for our entrance into the magic realms. On Commencement night we whispered merrily among ourselves on the stage to see our favorite planet, Venus, of course, smiling at us through a high, open window, "bidding adieu to her astronomy class," we said.

Then you went away to plunge into the most brilliant whirl of society, and I stayed in the beautiful old city to work.

Bernard was very much *en evidence* those days. He liked you a great deal, because in school-girl parlance you were my "chum." You say,—thanks, no tea, it reminds me that I'm an old maid; you say you know what happiness means— maybe, but I don't think any living soul could experience the joy I felt in those days; it was absolutely painful at times.

Byron and his counterparts are ever dear to the womanly heart, whether young or old. Such a man was he, gloomy, misanthropical, tired of the world, with a few dozen broken love-affairs among his varied experiences. Of course, I worshipped him secretly, what romantic, silly girl of my age, would not, being thrown in such constant contact with him.

One day he folded me tightly in his arms, and said:

"Little girl, I have nothing to give you in exchange for that priceless love of yours but a heart that has already been at another's feet, and a wrecked life, but may I ask for it?"

"It is already yours," I answered. I'll draw the veil over the scene which followed; you know, you've "been there."

Then began some of the happiest hours that ever the jolly old sun beamed upon, or the love-sick moon clothed in her rays of silver. Deceived me? No, no. He admitted that the old love for Blanche was still in his heart, but that he had lost all faith and respect for her, and could nevermore be other than a friend. Well, I was fool enough to be content with such crumbs.

We had five months of happiness. I tamed down beautifully in that time,—even consented to adopt the peerless Blanche as a model. I gave up all my most ambitious plans and cherished schemes, because he disliked women whose names were constantly in the mouth of the public. In fact, I became quiet, sedate, dignified, renounced too some of my best and dearest friends. I lived, breathed, thought, acted only for him; for me there was but one soul in the universe— Bernard's. Still, for all the suffering I've experienced, I'd be willing to go through it all again just to go over those five months. Every day together, at nights on the lake-shore listening to the soft lap of the waters as the silver sheen of the moon spread over the dainty curled waves; sometimes in a hammock swinging among the trees talking of love and reading poetry. Talk about Heaven! I just think there can't he a better time among the angels.

But there is an end to all things. A violent illness, and his father relenting, sent for the wayward son. I will always believe he loved me, but he was eager to get home to his mother, and anxious to view Blanche in the light of their new relationship. We had a whole series of parting scenes,—tears and vows and kisses exchanged. We clung to each other after the regulation fashion, and swore never to forget, and to write every day. Then there was a final wrench. I went back to my old life—he, away home.

For a while I was content, there were daily letters from him to read; his constant admonitions to practice; his many little tokens to adore—until there came a change,—letters less frequent, more mention of Blanche and her love for him, less of his love for me, until the truth was forced upon me. Then I grew cold and proud, and with an iron will crushed and stamped all love for him out of my tortured heart and cried for vengeance.

Yes, quite melo-dramatic, wasn't it? It is a dramatic tale, though.

So I threw off my habits of seclusion and mingled again with men and women, and took up all my long-forgotten plans. It's no use telling you how I succeeded. It was really wonderful, wasn't it? It seems as though that fickle goddess, Fortune, showered every blessing, save one, on my path. Success followed success, triumph succeeded triumph. I was lionized, feted, petted, caressed by the social and literary world. You often used to wonder how I stood it in all those years. God knows; with the heart-sick weariness and the fierce loathing that possessed me, I don't know myself.

But, mind you, Eleanor, I schemed well. I had everything seemingly that humanity craved for, but I suffered, and by all the gods, I swore that he should suffer too. Blanche turned against him and married his brother. An unfortunate chain of circumstances drove him from his father's home branded as a forger. Strange, wasn't it? But money is a strong weapon, and its long arm reaches over leagues and leagues of land and water.

One day he found me in a distant city, and begged for my love again, and for mercy and pity. Blanche was only a mistake, he said, and he loved me alone, and so on. I remembered all his thrilling tones and tender glances, but they might have moved granite now sooner than me. He knelt at my feet and pleaded like a criminal suing for life. I laughed at him and sneered at his misery, and told him what he had done for my happiness, and what I in turn had done for his.

Eleanor, to my dying day, I shall never forget his face as he rose from his knees, and with one awful, indescribable look of hate, anguish and scorn, walked from the room. As he neared the door, all the old love rose in me like a flood, drowning the sorrows of past years, and overwhelming me in a deluge of pity. Strive as I did, I could not repress it; a woman's love is too mighty to be put down with little reasonings. I called to him in terror, "Bernard, Bernard!" He did not turn; gave no sign of having heard.

"Bernard, come back; I didn't mean it!"

He passed slowly away with bent head, out of the house and out of my life. I've never seen him since, never heard of him. Somewhere, perhaps on God's earth, he wanders out-cast, forsaken, loveless. I have my vengeance, but it is like Dead Sea fruit, all bitter ashes to the taste. I am a miserable, heart-weary wreck,—a woman with fame, without love.

"Vengeance is an arrow that often falleth and smiteth the hand of him that sent it."

IN OUR NEIGHBORHOOD

The Harts were going to give a party. Neither Mrs. Hart, nor the Misses Hart, nor the small and busy Harts who amused themselves and the neighborhood by continually falling in the gutter on special occasions, had mentioned this fact to anyone, but all the interested denizens of that particular square could tell by the unusual air of bustle and activity which pervaded the Hart domicile. Lillian, the æsthetic, who furnished theme for many spirited discussions, leaned airily out of the window; her auburn (red) tresses carefully done in curl papers. Martha, the practical, flourished the broom and duster with unwonted activity, which the small boys of the neighborhood, peering through the green shutters of the front door, duly reported to their mammas, busily engaged in holding down their respective door-steps by patiently sitting thereon.

Pretty soon, the junior Harts,—two in number—began to travel to and fro, soliciting the loan of a "few chairs," "some nice dishes," and such like things, indispensable to every decent, self-respecting party. But to all inquiries as to the use to which these articles were to be put, they only vouchsafed one reply, "Ma told us as we wasn't to tell, just ask for the things, that's all."

Mrs. Tuckley the dress-maker, brought her sewing out on

the front-steps, and entered a vigorous protest to her next-door neighbor.

"Humph," she sniffed, "mighty funny they can't say what's up. Must be something in it. Couldn't get none o' *my* things, and not invite *me!*"

"Did she ask you for any?" absent-mindedly inquired Mrs. Luke, shielding her eyes from the sun.

"No-o—, but she'd better sense, she knows *me*—she ain't—mercy me, Stella! Just look at that child tumbling in the mud! You, Stella, come here, I say! Look at you now, there—and there—and there?"

The luckless Stella having been soundly cuffed, and sent whimpering in the back-yard, Mrs. Tuckley continued,

"Yes as I was saying, 'course, taint none o' my business, but I always did wonder how them Harts do keep up. Why, them girls dress just as fine as any lady on the Avenue and that there Lillian wears real diamond ear-rings. 'Pears mighty, mighty funny to me, and Lord the airs they do put on! Holdin' up their heads like nobody's good enough to speak to. I don't like to talk about people, you know yourself, Mrs. Luke, I never speak about anybody, but mark my word, girls that cut up capers like them Hartses' girls never come to any good."

Mrs. Luke heaved a deep sigh of appreciation at the wisdom of her neighbor, but before she could reply a re-inforcement in the person of little Mrs. Peters, apron over her head, hands shrivelled and soap-sudsy from washing, appeared.

"Did you ever see the like?" she asked in her usual, rapid breathless way. "Why, my Louis says they're putting canvass cloths on the floor, and taking down the bed in the back-room; and putting greenery and such like trash about. Some style about them, eh?"

Mrs. Tuckley tossed her head and sniffed contemptuously, Mrs. Luke began to rehearse a time worn tale, how once a carriage had driven up to the Hart house at nine o'clock at night, and a distinguished looking man alighted, went in, stayed about ten minutes and finally drove off with a great clatter. Heads that had shaken ominously over this story before began to shake again, and tongues that had wagged themselves tired with conjectures started now with some brand new ideas and theories. The children of the square, tired of fishing for minnows in the ditches, and making mud-pies in the street, clustered about their mother's skirts receiving occasional slaps, when their attempts at taking part in the conversation became too pronounced.

Meanwhile, in the Hart household, all was bustle and preparation. To and fro the members of the house flitted, arranging chairs, putting little touches here and there, washing saucers and glasses, chasing the Hart Juniors about, losing things and calling frantically for each other's assistance to find them. Mama Hart, big, plump, and perspiring, puffed here and there like a large, rosy engine, giving impossible orders, and receiving sharp answers to foolish questions. Lillian, the æsthetic, practiced her most graceful poses before the large mirror in the parlor; Martha rushed about, changing the order of the furniture, and Papa Hart, just come in from work, paced the rooms disconsolately, asking for dinner.

"Dinner!" screamed Mama Hart, "Dinner, who's got time to fool with dinner this evening? Look in the sideboard and you'll see some bread and ham; eat that and shut up."

Eight o'clock finally arrived, and with it, the music and some straggling guests. When the first faint chee-chee of the violin floated out into the murky atmosphere, the smaller portion of the neighborhood went straightway into ecstasies.

Boys and girls in all stages of deshabille clustered about the door-steps and gave vent to audible exclamations of approval or disapprobation concerning the state of affairs behind the green shutters. It was a warm night and the big round moon sailed serenely in a cloudless, blue sky. Mrs. Tuckley had put on a clean calico wrapper, and planted herself with the indomitable Stella on her steps, "to watch the purceedings."

The party was a grand success. Even the intensely critical small fry dancing on the pavement without to the scraping and fiddling of the string band, had to admit that. So far as they were concerned it was all right, but what shall we say of the guests within? They who glided easily over the canvassed floors, bowed, and scraped and simpered, "just like the big folks on the Avenue," who ate the ice-cream and cake, and drank the sweet, weak Catawba wine amid boisterous healths to Mr. and Mrs. Hart and the Misses Hart; who smirked and perspired and cracked ancient jokes and heart-rending puns during the intervals of the dances, who shall say that they did not enjoy themselves as thoroughly and as fully as those who frequented the wealthier entertainments up-town.

Lillian and Martha in gossamer gowns of pink and blue flitted to and fro attending to the wants of their guests. Mrs. Hart, gorgeous in a black satin affair, all folds and lace and drapery, made desperate efforts to appear cool and collected—and failed miserably. Papa Hart spent one half his time standing in front of the mantle, spreading out his coat-tails, and benignly smiling upon the young people, while the other half was devoted to initiating the male portion of the guests into the mysteries of "snake killing."

Everybody had said that he or she had had a splendid time, and finally, when the last kisses had been kissed, the last good-byes been said, the whole Hart family sat down in the now deserted and disordered rooms, and sighed with relief that the great event was over at last.

"Nice crowd, eh?" remarked Papa Hart. He was brimful of joy and second-class whiskey, so no one paid any attention to him.

"But did you see how shamefully Maude flirted with Willie Howard?" said Lillian. Martha tossed her head in disdain; Mr. Howard she had always considered her especial property, so Lillian's observation had a rather disturbing effect.

"I'm so warm and tired," cried Mama Hart, plaintively, "children, how are we going to sleep to-night?"

Thereupon the whole family arose to devise ways and means for wooing the drowsy god. As for the Hart Juniors they had long since solved the problem by falling asleep with sticky hands and faces upon a pile of bed-clothing behind the kitchen door.

—

It was late in the next day before the house had begun to resume anything like its former appearance. The little Harts were kept busy all morning returning chairs and dishes, and distributing the remnants of the feast to the vicinity. The ice-cream had melted into a warm custard, and the cakes had a rather worse for wear appearance, but they were appreciated as much as though just from the confectioner. No one was forgotten, even Mrs. Tuckley, busily stitching on a muslin garment on the steps, and unctuously rolling the latest morsel of scandal under her tongue, was obliged to confess that "them Hartses wasn't such bad people after all, just a bit queer at times."

About two o'clock, just as Lillian was re-draping the tidies on the stiff, common plush chairs in the parlor, some one pulled the bell violently. The visitor, a rather good-looking young fellow, with a worried expression, smiled somewhat sarcastically as he heard a sound of scuffling and running within the house.

———

Presently Mrs. Hart opened the door wiping her hand, red and smoking with dish-water, upon her apron. The worried expression deepened on the visitor's face as he addressed the woman with visible embarrassment.

"Er—I—I—suppose you are Mrs. Hart?" he inquired awkwardly.

"That's my name, sir," replied she with pretentious dignity.

"Er—your-er—may I come in madam?"

"Certainly," and she opened the door to admit him, and offered a chair.

"Your husband is an employee in the Fisher Oil Mills, is he not?"

Mrs. Hart straightened herself with pride as she replied in the affirmative. She had always been proud of Mr. Hart's position as foreman of the big oil mills, and was never so happy as when he was expounding to some one in her presence, the difficulties and intricacies of machine-work.

"Well you see, my dear Mrs. Hart," continued the visitor. "Now pray don't get excited—there has been an accident, and your husband—has—er—been hurt, you know."

But for a painful whitening in her usually rosy face, and a quick compression of her lips, the wife made no sign.

"What was the accident?" she queried, leaning her elbows on her knees.

"Well, you see, I don't understand machinery and the like, but there was something about a wheel out of gear, and a band bursted, or something, anyhow a big wheel flew to pieces, and as he was standing near, he was hit."

"Where?"

"Well—well, I may as well tell you the truth, madam; a large piece of the wheel struck him on the head—and—he was killed instantly."

She did not faint, nor make any outcry, nor tear her hair as he had partly expected, but sat still staring at him, with a sort of helpless, dumb horror shining out her eyes, then with a low moan, bowed her head on her knees and shuddered, just as Lillian came in, curious to know what the handsome stranger had to say to her mother.

—

The poor mutilated body came home at last, and was laid in a stiff, silver-decorated, black coffin in the middle of the sitting-room, which had been made to look as uncomfortable and unnatural as mirrors and furniture shrouded in sheets and mantel and tables divested of ornaments would permit.

There was a wake that night to the unconfined joy of the neighbors, who would rather a burial than a wedding. The friends of the family sat about the coffin, and through the house with long pulled faces. Mrs. Tuckley officiated in the kitchen, making coffee and dispensing cheese and crackers to those who were hungry. As the night wore on, and the first restraint disappeared, jokes were cracked, and quiet laughter indulged in, while the young folks congregated in the kitchen, were hilariously happy, until some member of the family would appear, when every face would sober down.

The older persons contented themselves with recounting the virtues of the deceased, and telling anecdotes wherein he figured largely. It was astonishing how many intimate friends of his had suddenly come to light. Every other man present had either attended school with him, or was a close companion until he died. Proverbs and tales and witty sayings were palmed off as having emanated from his lips. In fact, the dead man would have been surprised himself, had he suddenly come to life and discovered what an important, what a modern solomon he had become.

The long night dragged on, and the people departed in groups of twos and threes, until when the gray dawn crept slowly over the blackness of night shrouding the electric lights in mists of cloudy blue, and sending cold chills of dampness through the house, but a few of the great crowd remained.

The day seemed so gray in contrast to the softening influence of the night, the grief which could be hidden then, must now come forth and parade itself before all eyes. There was the funeral to prepare for; the dismal black dresses and bonnets with their long crape veils to don; there were the condolences of sorrowing friends to receive; the floral offerings to be looked at. The little Harts strutted about resplendent in stiff black cravats, and high crape bands about their hats. They were divided between two conflicting emotions— joy at belonging to a family so noteworthy and important, and sorrow at the death. As the time for the funeral approached, and Lillian began to indulge in a series of fainting fits, the latter feeling predominated.

—

Well it was all over at last, the family had returned, and as on two nights previous, sat once more in the deserted and dismantled parlor. Mrs. Tuckley and Mrs. Luke, having rendered all assistance possible, had repaired to their respective front steps to keep count of the number of visitors who returned to condole with the family.

"A real nice funeral," remarked the dress-maker at last, "a nice funeral. Everybody took it so hard, and Lillian fainted real beautiful. She's a good girl that Lillian. Poor things, I wonder what they'll do now."

Stella, the irrepressible, was busily engaged balancing herself on one toe, *à la* ballet.

"Mebbe she's goin' to get married," she volunteered eagerly, "'cos I saw that yeller-haired young man what comes there all the time, wif his arms around her waist, and a tellin' her not to grieve as he'd take care of her. I was a peepin' in the dinin'-room."

"How dare you peep at other folks, and pry into people's affairs? I can't imagine where you get your meddlesome ways from. There aint none in *my family*. Next time I catch you at it, I'll spank you good." Then, after a pause, "Well what else did he say?"

THE BEE-MAN

We were glancing over the mental photograph album, and commenting on the great lack of dissimilarity in tastes. Nearly every one preferred spring to any other season, with a very few exceptions in favor of autumn. The women loved Mrs. Browning and Longfellow; the men showed decided preferences after Emerson and Macauley. Conceit stuck out when the majority wanted to be themselves and none other, and only two did not want to live in the 19th century. But in one place, in answer to the question, "Whom would you rather be, if not yourself?" the answer was,

"A baby!"

"Why would you rather be a baby than any other personage?" queried someone glancing at the writer, who blushed as she replied.

"Because then I might be able to live a better life, I might have better opportunities and better chances for improving them, and it would bring me nearer the 20th century."

"About eight or nine years ago," said the first speaker, "I remember reading a story in a magazine for young folks. It was merely a fairy story, and perhaps was not intended to point a moral, but only to amuse the little ones. It was something on this order:—"

Once upon a time, there lived in an out of the way spot an

ancient decrepit Bee-man. How old he was no one knew; whence he came, no one could tell: to the memory of the oldest inhabitant he had always lived in his dirty hut, surrounded by myriads of hives, attended always by a swarm of bees. He was good to the bits of children, and always ready with a sweet morsel of honeycomb for them. All his ambitions, sympathies, and hopes were centered in his hives; until one day a fairy crept into his hut and whispered:

"You have not always been a common bee-man. Once you were something else."

"Tell me what I was," he asked eagerly.

"Nay, that I cannot do," replied the fairy, "our queen sent me to tell you this, and if you wished to search for your former self, I am to assist you. You must search the entire valley, and the first thing you meet to which you become violently attached, that is what you formerly were, and I shall give you back your correct form."

So the next morning the Bee-man, strapping his usual hive upon his back, and accompanied by the fairy in the form of a queen bee, set out upon his search throughout the valley. At first he became violently attached to the handsome person and fine castle of the Lord of the Realm, but on being kicked out of the lord's domains, his love turned to dislike.

The Bee-man and the fairy travelled far and wide and carefully inspected every thing they met. The very Imp, the Languid young man, the Hippogriffith, the Thousand Tailed Hippopotamus, and many other types, until the Bee-man grew weary and was about to give up the search in disgust.

But suddenly amid all the vast halls of the enchanted domains through which they were wandering, there sounded shrieks and wails, and the inmates were thrown into the greatest confusion by the sight of the hideous hippogriffith dashing through, a million sparks emanating from his great eyes, his barbed tail waving high in the air, and holding in his talons a tiny infant.

Now, as soon as the Bee-man saw this, a great wave of sorrow and pity filled his breast, and he hastily followed the monster, arriving at his cave just in time to see him preparing to devour his prey. Madly dashing his hive of bees into the hippogriffith's face, and seizing the infant while the disturbed and angry bees stung and swarmed, the Bee-man rushed out followed by the Very Imp, the Languid young man, and the fairy, and made his way to the child's mother. Just as soon as the baby was safely restored, the Bee-man ruminated thoughtfully awhile and finally remarked to the fairy:

"Do you know of all the things I have met so far, I liked the baby best of all, so I think I must have been a baby once!"

"Right you are," assented the fairy, "I knew it before, but, of course, I couldn't tell. Now I shall change you into your former shape, but remember, you must try to be something better than a Bee-man."

The Bee-man promised and was instantly changed into a baby. The fairy inoculated him from harm with a bee-sting, and gave him to the rescued infant's mother.

Nearly a cycle passed by, and one day the fairy, having business in the valley, thought she would make inquiries concerning her protégé. In her way she happened to pass a little, low, curious hut, with many bee hives about it, and swarms of bees flying in and out. The fairy, tired as well as curious, peeped in and discovered an ancient man attending to the wants of his pets. Upon a closer inspection, she recognized her infant of years ago. He had become a bee-man again!

—

"It points a pretty little moral," said the Fatalist, "for it certainly proves that do what we will, we cannot get away from our natures. It was inherent in that man's nature to tend bees. Bee-ing was the occupation chosen for him by Fate, and had the beneficent Fairy changed him a dozen times, he would ultimately have gone to bee-ing in some form or other."

The Fatalist was doubtless right, for it seems as though the inherent things in our nature must come out. But if we want to dig deep into the child's story for metaphysical morals, does it not also uphold the theory of re-incarnation? the ancient bee-man perhaps is but a type of humanity growing old, and settled in its mode of living, while the fairy is but thought, whispering into our souls things half dread half pleasant.

There are moments when the consciousness of a former life comes sharply upon us, in swift, lightning flashes, too sudden to be tangible, too dazzling to leave an impress, or mayhap, in troubled dreams that bewilder and confuse with vague remembrances. If only a burst of memory would come upon some mortal, that the tale might be fully told, and these theories established as facts. It would unfold great possibilities of historical lore; of literary life; of religious speculation.

ABOUT THE AUTHOR

ALICE DUNBAR-NELSON (1875–1935) was a writer of poems, short stories, and essays, as well as a journalist and an activist. A woman of African American, Anglo, Native American, and Creole heritage, Dunbar-Nelson was born in New Orleans, was an activist for African American and women's rights in the 1920s and 1930s, and became a key figure in the Harlem Renaissance. She was married three times, first to famous poet Paul Dunbar, then, after Dunbar's death, to doctor Henry A. Callis, and lastly to civil rights activist Robert J. Nelson. Throughout her life she also had romantic relationships with women, including Howard High School principal Edwina Kruse and journalist Fay M. Jackson. Dunbar-Nelson's writing often engaged with topics of racism, sexism, and sexuality, drawing on her experiences as a bisexual, multiracial woman. She published two short story collections, *Violets and Other Tales* in 1895 and *The Goodness of St. Rocque and Other Stories* in 1899, and wrote until her death in 1935.

ABOUT THE TYPE

The principal text of this Modern Library edition was set in a digitized version of Janson, a typeface that dates from about 1690 and was cut by Nicholas Kis (1650–1702), a Hungarian working in Amsterdam. The original matrices have survived and are held by the Stempel foundry in Germany. Hermann Zapf (1918–2015) re-designed some of the weights and sizes for Stempel, basing his revisions on the original design.